LUCKY LOSER

Visit us at www.boldstrokesbooks.com

By the Author

In Medias Res

Rum Spring

Lucky Loser

LUCKY LOSER

by
Yolanda Wallace

2011

LUCKY LOSER

ISBN 10: 1-60282-575-0
ISBN 13: 978-1-60282-575-8

This Trade Paperback Original Is Published By
Bold Strokes Books, Inc.
P.O. Box 249
Valley Falls, NY 12185

First Edition: November 2011

Credits
Editor: Cindy Cresap
Production Design: Susan Ramundo
Cover Design By Sheri (graphicartist2020@hotmail.com)

Acknowledgments

The first tennis match I ever saw was the 1981 US Open women's final between Martina Navratilova and Tracy Austin. I didn't know anything about the sport or its stars at the time, but I found myself rooting for the player the rest of the crowd seemed to be rooting against. Martina lost the hard-fought match in a third set tiebreaker, but her tears afterward endeared her to the crowd and to me. On that day, a lifelong tennis fan was born.

Lucky Loser was a labor of love for me, a chance to relive fond tennis memories while inventing some of my own. I hope you enjoy reading the book as much as I enjoyed writing it.

Thanks, as always, to my favorite doubles team—Radclyffe and the Bold Strokes family. Ladies, you're the best in the business. Dita, thank you for not laughing too hard when I played DVDs of classic tennis matches for research and invested myself in the outcomes as if the matches were live instead of twenty-five years old. And thank you most of all to the readers. You're aces.

Dedication

To Dita. You've made ten years seem more like ten minutes.
Game, set, match.

WARM UP

New York City

Sinjin Smythe bounced the ball once. Twice. Three times. She needed a big serve and she needed it now.

"Come on, Viktoriya! You can do it!"

A fan's cry of support for her opponent forced Sinjin to step away from the service line. She scrubbed her sweat-soaked wristband across her forehead then extended her hand to the ball boy. "Towel." As she dried her hands on the oversized red, white, and blue cloth, she took a moment to gather herself.

"Come on. Focus," she said under her breath. "This is the reason you moved four thousand miles away from home. This is the reason you left college after your junior year. To play and win Grand Slam finals."

Only she wasn't winning.

She looked around cavernous Arthur Ashe Stadium, the vast arena that was the largest stage in tennis. She had surprised herself—and the tennis cognoscenti who felt grass was her best surface—by making a spirited run to the final of the U.S. Open. The lucrative New York-based event was the last of the tennis season's four majors. The stars were out, literally and figuratively, for the prime-time final. And Sinjin, who had defeated four seeded players on her way to the championship match, was on the verge of losing in straight sets.

She could already imagine the headlines. The British press, ravenous for a champion of their own, had spent the past few years making her seem like Wonder Woman. In a few minutes, they would stop building her up and begin tearing her down. She had played the best tennis of her life in her run to the final, giving her nation's long-suffering sports fans hope she could translate her collegiate success to the professional ranks. Her stellar play had continued in the championship match, but her opponent had played the big points better. Too bad her hometown press wouldn't see it that way. If she went on to lose, the loss would be chalked up to a failure on her part, not attributed to her opponent's superior play.

Viktoriya Vasilyeva, the twenty-year-old Russian beauty with the long blond hair and even longer line of drooling fans, had won the first set 7-5 and was up 5-4 in the second. She was a point away from fulfilling every tennis player's dream. She was a point away from winning her first Grand Slam title.

Sinjin tossed her towel to the ball boy and tried to avoid having her dream turn into a nightmare. The sellout crowd of twenty-three thousand, which had spent most of the nearly two-hour match either on its feet or on the edge of its seat, held its collective breath.

Sinjin looked across the net at her foe. Viktoriya dried her racquet hand on the hem of her stylish black tennis dress as she prowled the baseline. Desire seeped out of every pore. Her will to win was nearly as intimidating as her power-packed game. But nothing—not even one of Viktoriya's turbo-powered ground strokes—was as intimidating as Sinjin's serve. When her serve was on, she could do anything. She could beat anyone. Anyone except Viktoriya.

Sinjin's flashy serve-and-volley game was built on aggression. She overwhelmed her opponents with constant pressure. She employed the same tactics now, hitting a powerful first serve and following it to the net.

Up to the task, Viktoriya lashed a wickedly angled return. Sinjin dove for the ball but came up empty. Just like she always seemed to when she played Viktoriya. They had played each other dozens of times over the years, first in the junior ranks and now in the pros. Sinjin had yet to record a victory. Their latest encounter was no different.

"Game, set, match, Vasilyeva," the chair umpire said. "Vasilyeva wins two sets to love."

Viktoriya's stern game face vanished the instant the ball passed out of Sinjin's reach. She squealed in delight and tossed her racquet high in the air as the crowd roared its approval.

On the other side of the net—and the other end of the spectrum—Sinjin lay on her back and stared at the night sky. Chances to win Grand Slam singles titles—to etch your name in the annals of sports history—didn't come along every day. Some players went their entire careers without ever reaching a Grand Slam final. She had made it in her first year. But she had blown her opportunity. Would it be her only one?

Viktoriya leaped across the net and helped Sinjin to her feet. "I'm sorry it had to be you," she said, draping an arm across Sinjin's shoulder. Her once-impenetrable Russian accent was so slight it was almost undetectable. Years of living in the States made her sound like a native, not a visitor.

"It sucks to make it this far and lose, but at least I lost to a better player. You deserved it. Congratulations."

"Thanks, Sinjin. That means a lot coming from you."

Sinjin plastered on a smile she forced to remain in place throughout the seemingly endless trophy presentation. She didn't want her dissatisfaction with her loss to detract from Viktoriya's joy over her win. Viktoriya had finally lived up to the expectations that had been heaped on her since she was seven. When her parents had sold everything they owned to buy three tickets from Moscow to Orlando, Florida, so she could train at an elite tennis academy. She had finally made their sacrifice a success instead of a foolish gamble. She had earned the right to enjoy the moment.

Sinjin remembered to thank all the sponsors during her runner-up speech, and she tried to look happy when a string of bigwigs presented Viktoriya with a check for a million dollars, the keys to a new Lexus, and the silver trophy most players would give an eyetooth to hold aloft. Once she reached the locker room, Sinjin afforded herself the luxury of a good cry.

Viktoriya, showered and changed and on her way to a press conference, paused to offer a few words of consolation. "We used to dream about this when we were kids," she said, sitting next to her. "Remember when we were at the academy and we would pretend our practice sessions were the finals of Wimbledon or the U.S. Open?"

Sinjin nodded. "You always won those sessions, so I guess I shouldn't be surprised you won this one, too."

The women's tennis tour was as cutthroat as any big business, but some players allowed themselves to cultivate friendships, making a life largely spent on the road a little less lonely.

Sinjin and Viktoriya had known each other since they were teenagers. Even though Viktoriya was two years younger, she had more experience as a professional. She had joined the tour shortly after her sixteenth birthday. Sinjin had completed three years of college before turning pro. While Sinjin had worried about class loads and keg parties, Viktoriya had fretted over ranking points and endorsement opportunities. Sinjin was the late bloomer. Viktoriya was the prodigy. Now she had gone from being a phenom to a champion. Sinjin was still waiting for her chance to do the same.

Viktoriya rested her chin on Sinjin's shoulder. "Let me buy you dinner," she said, twirling one of Sinjin's dreadlocks around her finger. "Would that make you feel better?"

"I thought it was my turn to pay."

Grinning, Viktoriya fanned herself with her victor's check. "I think I can afford it better than you can."

Sinjin dried her eyes. "In that case, let's find the most expensive restaurant in town."

"How about my hotel? The room service is excellent, and I wouldn't have to share you with anyone."

"Except for your parents and your agent and your coach and your trainer and—"

"Not tonight. Tonight, the only person I want to celebrate with is you." Viktoriya trailed her fingertips across Sinjin's forearm, causing the fine hairs to stand on end. "I can almost feel your long, chiseled legs wrapped around me. I can practically see you with your head thrown back, your mouth open in a silent scream of ecstasy as I lick your caramel-colored skin and thrust my fingers deep inside your silken folds."

Sinjin took a long look at Viktoriya. "I don't remember this being a part of our conversations at the academy."

"That's because it was part of my fantasies. Will you help me turn my fantasies into reality?"

Sinjin considered the question for a split-second. "Where are you staying?"

❖

Sinjin slipped the key card into the lock and waited for the light to turn green. Then she opened the door and stepped into the room.

The lights were turned down low. Soft music gently played on the stereo system.

Viktoriya had booked a suite at the Ritz-Carlton, though not in her own name. "For privacy's sake," she had said, but Sinjin thought the subterfuge might have more to do with the bottle of Dom Pérignon that sat chilling in a sterling silver ice bucket. Viktoriya might be the queen of the tennis world, but in the country of her ascension to the throne, she was still too young to drink.

Pocketing the key card she had picked up from the front desk, Sinjin looked around the suite. The expansive space included an entry foyer, two living rooms, two bathrooms, a marble tub, seven hundred thread count sheets, and a dining room that seated eight. Sinjin whistled in appreciation of the luxe surroundings. The nightly room rate was four times more than her monthly rent.

Treating herself to a bottle of mineral water from the minibar, she waited for Viktoriya. And waited. And waited.

Two hours later, after the ice had melted and Sinjin's ardor had cooled, Viktoriya finally arrived. In her trench coat and black sunglasses, she looked like a Cold War-era spy.

"I'm sorry I'm late. The press wouldn't let me leave." She placed two oversized shopping bags in the nearest chair and kicked off her designer shoes. A diamond-encrusted tennis bracelet circled her wrist.

Sinjin eyed the shopping bags. "I didn't know the press conducted interviews at Niemen Marcus."

"You know how it is." Viktoriya opened the champagne and poured two glasses. She extended one toward Sinjin. "I'm so glad you stayed."

Sinjin drained the proffered glass then looked pointedly at her watch. "And now I have to go."

"Why? I just got here."

"That's nice, but I have a match to play tomorrow. If everything goes well, you won't be the only one leaving New York with a Grand Slam title under her belt."

Viktoriya rolled her eyes and took a sip of champagne. "No one cares about doubles. No one except for tennis fanatics and players who aren't good enough to make an impact in singles."

Sinjin's temper flared. For the doubles final, she would be partnered with Laure Fortescue, the French player who was the only other out lesbian on tour. Their finals opponents were an unseeded team who had upset the Williams sisters in the semifinals. Long shots when the tournament began, Sinjin and Laure entered the final as the favorites.

They had nicknamed themselves the Rainbow Brigade, though one tour official, hyperaware of the assumptions casual fans made about female athletes, had asked them not to publicize the fact. Or to, as he put it, "broadcast" their lesbianism. Instead of retreating into the closet, Sinjin and Laure had smashed its doors down, opting to play with colorful gay pride bracelets on their wrists.

They had been playing together for only a few months, but Sinjin wondered how long it would be before their commitment to singles would end their doubles partnership. Hadn't the same thing happened to the teams of Evert-Navratilova and Graf-Sabatini?

"I care," she said. "So does my partner. I might not be top ten material just yet, but the last time I looked, Laure was in the top five."

"Not for long. When the rankings come out on Monday, I'm going to be number five and she's going to drop to six. By this time next year, I'm going to be number one. Everyone's going to be looking up at me, including Laure. But right now, I'd rather look up at you." Viktoriya wrapped her arm around Sinjin's waist and licked the side of her neck. "Mmm. If your skin is this good, I can't wait to see what the rest of you tastes like."

Sinjin disengaged Viktoriya's arm and gently pushed her away. "It might be *just* doubles, but it still looks good on a résumé. So if you will excuse me—"

Viktoriya blocked Sinjin's escape route. "I'm sorry if what I said came out the wrong way. There's good money to be made in doubles. And a title is a title, whether it's won on your own or with a partner. But you didn't come over here to talk about tennis, did you?"

Viktoriya unbuttoned her trench coat and let it fall to the floor. The sight of her toned, six-foot-two body in lacy black lingerie silenced Sinjin's protests.

Viktoriya smiled triumphantly. "I didn't think so."

Sinjin picked Viktoriya up and carried her to the bed. After Sinjin laid her down, Viktoriya spread her legs as if she were daring Sinjin to claim her prize.

Sinjin kissed Viktoriya's full lips and moved lower. Past the perfect breasts. Over the flat stomach. Her mouth grazed Viktoriya's mound and closed around her warm, wet center. She painted the hood of Viktoriya's clit with long, slow strokes then flicked her tongue at the bundle of nerves at the tip.

Viktoriya groaned deep in her throat and buried her hands in Sinjin's hair. Her hips matched Sinjin's rhythm as Sinjin licked and sucked her clit. She squeezed her eyes shut. "Fuck," she said through gritted teeth as her head thrashed against the pillow. The muscles in her well-defined thighs and calves flexed and released. Flexed and released.

Sinjin brushed her fingertips along Viktoriya's sensitive inner thighs. Viktoriya groaned again. Sinjin loved the moment of submission, the moment of pure acquiescence when a woman she was with let everything else go and completely gave herself over to pleasure and sensation. Her once-perfect hair mussed, her skin mottled, her breath coming in short, ragged bursts, Viktoriya had reached that moment. When Sinjin reached up and gently squeezed her nipples, Viktoriya nearly launched herself off the bed.

"Now. Take me now."

The hoarse whisper drove Sinjin wild.

She slipped two fingers inside Viktoriya's smooth walls. With her left hand, she reached down and tended to her own need. When Viktoriya's cries of release began, so did hers. Viktoriya's muscles spasmed around her fingers, drawing them deeper inside. Her own clit twitched and pulsed against her hand. She heaved a satisfied sigh and rolled off.

"Now," Viktoriya said, "wasn't that worth waiting for?"

Laure Fortescue fiddled with her racquets. She straightened the strings, checked the tension, and rewrapped the grips. She didn't know what was strung tighter, the racquets or her. She checked her watch for the umpteenth time. Sinjin was late. Very late. They were due on court in ten minutes. If Sinjin didn't show up soon, they would be defaulted. Laure would rather play and get beaten love and love than lose without even taking the court.

A few minutes later, Sinjin ran into the locker room spouting apologies—and excuses.

"I know you're probably pissed, but hear me out. First, I overslept. Then I had a hard time hailing a cab. When I finally got one to stop, we ran into the world's worst traffic jam. After sitting at a standstill for ten minutes, I tossed the driver twenty bucks, got out of the car, and hoofed it. I won't need the ten-minute warm-up because I just ran three miles."

Sinjin finally took a breath. Then she flashed the smile that had melted women's hearts all over the globe.

"How was your day?" she asked, quickly changing out of her street clothes into her tennis attire.

"Better than yours."

Laure stowed her racquets in the bulky, oversized bag that also contained an extra set of clothes, an mp3 player, assorted protein-laden snacks, and the battered silver loving cup she carried for luck. The tiny trophy was the first she had ever won. She had earned it at a junior tournament in Paris when, as a twelve-year-old, she had beaten a string of more heralded players three and four years her senior. The trophy was a tangible reminder that although she might be overlooked because of her relatively small size, her all-court game wouldn't let her be forgotten.

"I called you after the final last night, but you didn't pick up," she said as Sinjin leaned over to tie her shoes. "What happened to you?"

"Viktoriya Vasilyeva."

Laure frowned. "Is she the one who gave you those boulders in your ears?"

Sinjin touched one of the diamond studs weighing down her lobes. "She bought them for herself, but she decided they looked better on me." She zipped her warm-up jacket. "You're not jealous, are you?"

"Hardly." Laure pulled a racquet out of her bag and pantomimed a few ground strokes. "I'm a firm believer that one should never take relationship advice from someone who isn't in a relationship. So feel free to take what I say next with a grain of salt. Do what makes you happy, Sin, but be careful. Viktoriya's more trouble than she's worth."

"What do you mean?"

Laure swung at another invisible ball. "You'll see." She looked up when the opposing team approached. Emme Wechselberger kept walking, but Abby McGuinness lingered to talk.

"I'm glad you could make it, Sin. Laure and I were starting to think you couldn't be arsed to show up." Abby's lilting Irish accent and broad smile took the bite out of her words. "Okay, maybe that was a bit of wishful thinking on my part. No matter who comes out on top today, you and I will give the home folks a reason to lay the tea and crumpets aside, eh? After the match, what do you say we get together and tip a pint to our success?"

Sinjin slung her racquet bag over her shoulder. "Loser buys the first round."

"Then I guess the first round's going to be on you." Abby turned to Laure. "You're welcome to join us if you like."

"Thanks for the invitation, but I don't like to crash private parties."

"You should. It might turn that perpetual frown of yours upside down."

"See?" Sinjin said after Abby left. "I'm not the only one who's noticed you've become a nun."

Laure felt her cheeks redden. "I haven't been out of the dating game that long," she said as they made the long walk from the locker room to the tunnel that led to stadium court.

"Why are you out of the dating game in the first place when there are *so* many women who would love to hear you whisper sweet nothings to them in that sexy accent of yours?"

"I'm looking for Miss Right not Miss Right Now."

Applause greeted Abby and Emme as they exited the tunnel and walked on court. Laure waited to be introduced.

"You're not going to find her either if you're too busy playing and practicing to search," Sinjin said.

"Says the woman who's too busy running from traffic jams to warm up for her match."

"Are you going to hold that against me for the rest of our lives?"

Laure playfully snapped the rainbow-colored rubber bracelet on Sinjin's wrist. "Only if we lose."

They walked out of the tunnel together, waving in unison to the surprisingly large crowd.

Ninety minutes later, Laure prepared to serve for the match. She and Sinjin had gotten off to a sluggish start, losing the first three games before they fought back to win the first set in a tiebreaker. The second set was more routine. Up 7-6, 5-2, they held double championship point.

"Forgive me yet?" Sinjin asked as they huddled at the baseline.

In the stands, a large group of fans in colorful tie-dyed shirts began a rhythmic chant. "Let's go, Rainbow!"

Laure tried not to smile. "Ask me after we win the next point."

She loved playing doubles. Singles garnered more attention and drew larger crowds, but the camaraderie of doubles was unmatched and the fans were much more vocal. Sinjin, though her behavior could be maddening at times, was the best doubles partner she had ever had. If Sinjin played every singles match the way she had when she'd decimated her in the semifinals, everyone on tour would be in trouble.

Sinjin covered her mouth to keep Abby and Emme from reading her lips as she and Laure discussed strategy. "Where are you going with this next serve, out wide or down the middle?"

Laure raised a ball to her lips. "Out wide."

"Are you sure? The last time you served wide to Abby, she punished us with one of her killer forehands."

"I know."

"Then why play with fire?"

Laure's competitive pride kicked in. "Because I dare her to hit two in a row."

"Whatever you say, partner. I'll let you know if I'm going to poach or stay home."

Sinjin slapped Laure's palm, then skipped to the net. Laure waited for her signal. After Abby and Emme assumed their return positions, Sinjin held one hand behind her back. Her fingers were crossed, indicating that if the return was in reach, she intended to enter Laure's half of the court to play it. If Abby's reply went down the line instead of crosscourt, Laure would have to hustle to cover the shot.

Laure hit her first serve at less than full strength to make sure she got the ball in play. The ball landed short and bounced toward the stands. The rubber soles of Abby's tennis shoes squeaked as she stretched to return the acutely angled shot. Sinjin sprinted to her right at the same time Laure sprinted to her left.

Abby barely got her racquet on the ball. Her return popped high into the air.

"Yours!" Laure called out as the ball drifted over the net.

Sinjin circled under the ball, setting up for an overhead. Then she squared her feet and let the ball bounce. She took aim at the wide gap between Abby and Emme, who watched helplessly as the incoming smash split their defenses.

Laure began to celebrate even before the ball landed. Running toward Sinjin, she raised her hand to give her a high five.

"Forgive me now?" Sinjin asked.

She swept Laure into her arms and kissed her. Laure froze, uncertain how to respond. She hated public displays of affection, but Sinjin's excitement was infectious. She laughed as Sinjin spun her in a delirious circle.

"I'm sorry I got carried away," Sinjin said after she lowered Laure to the ground, "but that's the happiest I've ever been. On court or off."

"I know what you mean." Laure's adrenaline was still pumping even after the trophy presentation. "Maybe I will join you and Abby tonight," she said as they headed to the locker room. "As long as I can have wine instead of beer."

Sinjin pulled her ringing cell phone out of her racquet bag and broke into a grin. "I'm going to have to give both of you a rain check, I'm afraid." She turned the phone so Laure could read the display.

Nicely done. Now get back over here ASAP. I want to see whose is bigger. And I'm not talking about trophies. V.

Laure cradled her latest trophy in the crook of her arm. "Have fun."

Sinjin flashed that lady-killer smile again. "Don't I always?"

Pre-Qualifying

London
Three Years Later

Sinjin stared out the bedroom window. The sky was bright blue. Not a cloud to be seen. She would have preferred one of the dreary mid-summer days England was known for. Overcast skies and constant, pissing rain would better suit her foul mood.

She had been off the tour for months. So long she had begun to wonder if she'd ever make it back.

She thought back on her career. She had made the U.S. Open final when she was twenty-two years old. A few months after that, she was firmly ensconced in the top twenty. The next year she had reached the top fifteen. Everything was as it was supposed to be. Then, just as she set her sights on the top ten, everything began to fall apart. She developed tendonitis in her knees, which slowed her approaches to the net and made her an easy target to pass. The losses began to mount. Her ranking, once as high as eleven, plummeted to the triple digits.

She tried everything. Rest. Ice. Even cutting back on doubles to save herself for singles. Nothing worked. The losses continued to pile up. Especially to Viktoriya. She seemed to draw Viktoriya in the first round of every tournament she qualified for, ensuring both an early exit and a substandard payday. Even though she could make Viktoriya scream like a banshee in bed, she couldn't win a match against her to save her life. And that was before she underwent the procedure she hoped would save her career. How would she fare now?

I'll probably be lucky to win a game.

As Viktoriya had predicted, she had soared to number one. Sinjin's ranking began with a one, too, but two more digits followed it. Relegated to the minor leagues, she fought for scraps while Viktoriya raked in millions. Sinjin's professional life was in disarray. Her personal life was, too. Her sister was in the other room, but she had never felt so alone. Where were the fans when she needed them? Where were the groupies now that she was on the verge of being a has-been instead of a sure thing? Who would she be if she couldn't be a tennis player?

She was scared. She would play again. Of that, she was sure. But would she be the same player she once was? Could she climb the mountain again or were her best days behind her?

She looked down at her damaged knees.

"Get well, will you? We've got work to do."

Stephanie stuck her head in the room. "Laure's on the phone. Is it safe for her to come over or are you in one of your moods?"

Sinjin tossed the latest get-well card into the growing pile. "I don't have moods."

"I'm sure you think your shite doesn't stink either, dear sister, but let me assure you you're wrong on both counts."

"Tell her to come over. I could use a *friendly* face."

Stephanie blew her a kiss. "Thanks, sis. I love you, too."

Sinjin smiled to herself after Stephanie closed the door. Even though she gave Steph a hard time, she couldn't live without her.

Maybe one day I'll meet someone who feels the same way about me.

❖

Laure held a bouquet of geraniums in one hand and a bottle of red wine in the other. "I didn't know whether to bring wine or flowers so I brought both."

Stephanie Smythe ushered Laure inside her apartment. The tastefully decorated flat in London's trendy Soho district was a stone's throw from the upscale clothing store where the budding fashionista worked as a window dresser.

Stephanie reached for the flowers. "Cute *and* courtly. Tell me again why you're still single."

"You sound like your sister."

"Is she playing matchmaker again?"

"More like assistant coach. We Skype each other a couple times a week. I'd rather talk about something other than tennis, but she always ends up trying to give me advice about where I should direct my serve on an important point or how many times I should approach the net during a match. If she keeps it up, she's going to give my real coach a run for his money."

"She misses the game."

"I miss her, too. We all do."

"Fingers crossed, she'll be back on court soon. Then she can stop giving me gray hair and give you career advice in person. If you ask me, I think she should audition for a different role in your life."

"Such as?"

"Girlfriend."

Laure shook her head as she examined a framed photo of Sinjin, Stephanie, and their mother. In the picture, the trio shared a bench and matching smiles. Sinjin looked adorable. She still did. But Laure had no interest in becoming the latest entry in her long list of one-night stands. "She and I make better friends than lovers."

"How would you know unless you tried?"

Laure touched a worn spot on a corner of the wooden frame. "What happened here?"

"Sin rubs the picture for luck before each match at Wimbledon. I keep telling her if she ever wins the tournament, she's going to have to buy me a new frame."

Stephanie strode to the kitchen. Laure followed, wondering how Stephanie made walking in six-inch heels look so easy. She could barely manage flats. "How's the patient?" she asked as Stephanie filled a vase with water.

"Grouchy." Stephanie arranged the flowers in the vase then ran her fingers through her wavy brown hair. Unlike Sinjin's hair, which stretched halfway down her back in layers of brown ropes, Stephanie's naturally curly hair had been straightened and cropped into a short, asymmetrical bob. "Maybe you can put a smile on her face because I certainly can't."

"Where is she?"

"In there." Stephanie jerked her head toward what Laure assumed was the bedroom. "I hope you brought a flak jacket. You might need it."

"Thanks for the warning." Laure tiptoed to the room Stephanie had indicated and rapped on the door. "Are you decent?"

The thick oak door muffled Sinjin's reply. "Unfortunately, yes."

"I come in peace." Laure opened the door wide enough for her arm to fit through the crack. She held out the bottle of wine. "I also come bearing gifts."

"Then get your arse in here."

Laure entered the room. Scores of get-well cards littered the bed where Sinjin lay crablike on her back. Laure had never seen her looking so vulnerable. Sinjin's muscular six-foot-one frame normally looked vibrant. Now she looked frail. Her hazel eyes lacked their usual luster. Her latte-colored skin was sallow.

Sinjin the Invincible looked defeated. She looked scared. She looked—for lack of a better word—human.

Laure tried to keep her expression neutral to hide her shock. She could tell by the look on Sinjin's face she had failed miserably. "I'm sorry," she said, bending to kiss Sinjin's cheeks, "but it's hard seeing you like this."

"Trust me. It's even harder being like this."

Laure pulled up a chair. "How are you?"

"Homesick."

"But you *are* home."

"Sometimes this doesn't feel like home. I haven't lived in England full-time since I was fifteen. I miss Miami."

"And your apartment with the two hundred seventy-degree view of the Atlantic Ocean? I can't blame you."

Sinjin looked wistful. "I want to sit on my balcony and soak up the sun with my feet on the railing and a beer in my hand."

"Sounds lovely. Would you like some company?"

"I thought you were more of a wine connoisseur than a beer fan."

"Living on a vineyard tends to do that to you, but I'm nothing if not flexible."

"So I've heard," Sinjin said with a rakish grin.

"You must not have heard that from Mireille. According to her, I'm a cold fish. I suppose that's why she was better at deflecting passes on the field than off."

"Don't listen to her. All those headers have made her loopy."

Laure had recently ended a two-year relationship with one of the strikers on France's women's national soccer team. Mireille had made her incredibly happy—when her infidelity wasn't making her miserable.

"Are you okay?" Sinjin asked.

"I'm getting there."

Sinjin held out her hand. Laure gave it a brief squeeze. She couldn't talk about Mireille for long without crying. When they were together, Mireille had made her feel like the only woman in the world. She had been devastated to discover she wasn't the only one, just one of many.

"So it's back to the nunnery for me," she said. "This time for good. There's room for one more if you care to join me."

"Only if you change some of the rules first. The one requiring celibacy really bites. I'm not crazy about the costumes either."

"I'll put in a word with the Mother Superior and get back to you."

Sinjin looked at the bottle of wine in Laure's hand. "Is that one of yours?"

Laure handed her the bottle. "Beaujolais nouveau. It's quite good, if I say so myself. In fact, I'm considering putting my racquets away and switching to winemaking."

"Laure Fortescue, professional vintner. I can see it." Sinjin placed the bottle on the nightstand next to the bed. "Shouldn't you be preparing for the French?"

Laure grimaced at the mention of the tournament that had caused her nothing but heartache over the years. The tournament she wanted to win more than any other. Not only would a win at the French Open give her the career Grand Slam, it would shut her critics up for good. The ones who called her a choker and questioned her nerves. Chokers, she liked to argue, didn't have three Grand Slam titles. Chokers didn't make it to number one in the world.

If she were to earn a French Open crown, three things would have to happen: she would have to play well, she would need to get a good draw, and she would have to have some help. Clay was her worst surface. She thought she might be able to knock off one of the top players on a given day, but not the two or three she would need to defeat in order to win the event. She hadn't given up hope, but she wasn't holding her breath either.

"I played Stuttgart and Rome and won a grand total of three matches. I'm tempted to ask the tournament organizers in Madrid to use one of their special exemptions and give me a wild card into the event even though I missed the entry deadline, but what's the point? I've played great going into Paris and lost early; I've played lousy beforehand and made the semifinals. Whatever happens happens. I've come to terms with it. The clay court season and I have a love-hate relationship. It loves to punish me and I hate to see that part of the calendar roll around. Maybe I should take a page from your book and wait for Wimbledon."

"Talk about jumping out of the frying pan into the fire."

Clay was the most forgiving surface to play on, but the long matches tested players' endurance. The French Open was played on slow red clay topped with a layer of crushed brick. After the two-week event ended, weary warriors had less than a month to prepare for their next test. And the next test was a stern one.

Wimbledon was a different animal from any other tournament. The event's physical challenge was daunting enough. The only major played on a living surface, Wimbledon's grass courts changed from year to year and even—depending on the weather—from day to day. By tournament's end, bad bounces wreaked havoc on rallies and bare patches made footing treacherous. At Wimbledon, where one court was nicknamed the Graveyard of Champions, the old saying that it was better to be lucky than good never applied more.

Despite those obstacles, at Wimbledon, the tennis itself was the easy part. Waiting out the rain delays, dealing with the backlog of matches caused by the dodgy weather, and being hounded by Fleet Street's numerous tabloid journalists was the hard part. Waiting hours—and sometimes days—to complete a match was tough enough. Throw in inflammatory headlines in the newspapers, inane questions in the press conferences, and unscrupulous reporters lurking in the shadows trying to manufacture controversy for the sake of a story, and it was tantamount to mental torture.

"Are you going to be able to play Wimbledon this year?" Laure asked.

"I'm going to use the qualifying tournament at Roehampton to see if I'm well enough to compete. If I qualify for Wimbledon, I'll play. But I'm not going to take a wild card. I don't want any handouts. Injury or no injury, I want to earn my spot."

If Sinjin wasn't accepting any of the spots set aside for promising young players and older ones attempting comebacks, that meant the Rainbow Brigade wouldn't be reuniting any time soon. Sinjin had cut back on her doubles the past couple of years to protect her balky knees. Laure rarely played doubles at all so she could concentrate on singles. Her singles ranking was in the top ten, but her doubles ranking was so low she and Sinjin wouldn't be able to enter the Wimbledon doubles tournament without qualifying. Laure couldn't afford to waste energy playing the quallies. Not when she had only one more shot at winning the Ladies' Plate.

"Your ranking isn't high enough to earn you direct entry into the singles? You've won two tournaments this year."

"Those were on the challenger circuit, where I had the distinct pleasure of calling my own lines, stealing fruit from the hospitality suite, and boarding with any generous family who would take me in because I couldn't afford a hotel room."

"What happened to your endorsement contracts?"

"I still have deals for racquets and strings, but my clothing company dumped me in April because I couldn't get my ranking back into the top fifty. A 'cost-cutting measure,' they called it. I was barely able to walk earlier this year, let alone win tennis matches. As for training, forget it. All I could do when I wasn't playing was manage the pain. After a while, even that wasn't enough. The tendonitis in my knees started getting worse, not better. I wanted to wait until the off-season to do something about it, but the way my body felt, there was no way I would have been able to make it to the off-season in one piece. Then I heard about PRP."

Laure grimaced again. PRP therapy was effective. Its recipients swore by it, but it sounded positively barbaric. During the procedure, doctors drew vials of patients' blood, separated it, and injected platelet-rich plasma directly into the affected tendons. Even if the treatment worked wonders as advertised, the thought of someone sticking needles into her knees gave Laure the creeps.

"For a while, I thought my career was over," Sinjin said. "It still might be, but at least I've given myself a chance. If the therapy works, I might be able to play for five more years. If not, you could see me in the broadcast booth in a couple of months."

Laure remembered all the late-night Skype sessions. "Or in the coaching ranks."

"No way," Sinjin said with a wink. "Tennis players are too hard to deal with. Haven't you heard? They're all divas and drama queens."

"Speak for yourself. I've never caused my coaches any sleepless nights."

"I would tell you to pull the other leg, but neither one is feeling too good right now."

"Are you taking anything for the pain?"

Sinjin moved around on the bed as if she were trying to find a more comfortable position. "There's a list of acceptable painkillers I could take, but I don't want to risk failing a drug test. You know how the rumor mill is. Even if the screw-up was the doctor's fault and I had a valid medical reason for taking what he gave me, I'd never be able to clear my name."

When Sinjin changed positions again, Laure fluffed the pillows under her knees. "How bad is the pain?" she asked, taking note of the fine sheen of sweat on Sinjin's forehead.

"On a scale of one to ten, it's about an eleven. My doctors warned me that the sites of the injections would be sore for up to a couple of weeks. They also said the 'discomfort' I felt prior to the procedure would worsen after it due to the increased fluid and pressure in the area. They conveniently forgot to mention the pain wouldn't be just a little bit worse but exponentially so. Some days I feel like an animal caught in a trap, tempted to chew my legs off in order to make the ache go away. But if it gets me back in the top twenty, I'm willing to bite the bullet."

Laure sifted through the get well cards on the bed. Some were from players. Most were from fans. All were from the many women who had shared Sinjin's bed over the years. Laure reached for another card. The illustration on the front of the card depicted Snoopy and Woodstock wearing headbands and tennis whites, vintage wooden racquets in their hands. The handwritten message inside the card read, *If you wanted to avoid losing to me yet again, my love, there are easier things you could have done—Viktoriya*. Laure held up the card. "Has she come to see you?"

Sinjin snorted. "Why would she?"

"You've been friends for ten years. You were lovers for—"

"We weren't lovers. Sex was a game for her. A way to get under my skin off the court so she could control me on it. I'm taking a page from your book. As long as I live, I will never sleep with another player."

"I'll believe that when I see it." Laure tossed the card back on the pile.

As a rule, she didn't date players, their coaches, or their trainers. The tour was too small and life was too short. She preferred to limit the drama to her matches and keep it as far away from her personal life as possible. Two ultra-competitive people in the same household didn't work. Mireille had helped her learn that lesson firsthand. Everything was a contest. Even sex felt like a race. Who could make who come faster. Who could hold out longer. She was ready to live life at her own pace. She was done with competing.

"Did you know Viktoriya hired David away from me?" Sinjin asked.

"Your coach? Viktoriya's number one in the world. Why would she change coaches?"

"Because it gave her a chance to screw with my head like she always does. When David called to tell me he was jumping ship, he said she told him I wasn't going to be using his services anytime soon and she didn't want his skills to go to waste."

"Are you looking for a new coach? I know Roger Federer played without one for a while, but he was a special case. His wife's a former player so he could talk strategy with her and he had enough people around him to put someone else in charge of making hotel reservations and booking departure times for his private jet. Who's going to do that for you?"

"The last time I looked, I was using public transportation, not private planes."

"You know what I mean. Who's going to handle the day-to-day stuff while you're grinding it out on the practice court?"

"I'll cross that bridge when I come to it. The first thing I have to do is find out if I can play. If I can't, the point is moot. If I can, I'm thinking of reaching out to Andrew Grey. He discovered me when I was a kid. He knows my game better than anyone. Even though he's retired now, I might be able to talk him into some kind of temporary arrangement until I can figure some things out." Sinjin picked up Viktoriya's card and flung it across the room. "Talk about rubbing salt in the wound." She ducked her head to meet Laure's downcast eyes. "I think this is the part where you're supposed to say, 'I told you so.'"

Laure squeezed her hand. "I'll wait until you're back on your feet. At the moment, it's just too easy."

Sinjin pulled away. "It's just a matter of time, you know. As soon as I'm healthy again, the groupies will come flocking back. And I'll welcome them with open arms." She smiled as if the statement were something to be proud of.

"Were you really thinking about quitting?"

"Not by choice. I fought tooth and nail to become a professional. I wasn't about to throw it away at the first sign of adversity. Out of the millions of people who play tennis, there are only one hundred who play it better than I do. For a while, that number was even smaller. With a bit of luck and a lot of hard work, it can be again. Tennis has been a part of my life for as long as I can remember. It's something I've done day in, day out for twenty years. It's all I've known since I was five years old. I'm a tennis player. That's all I've ever wanted to be. That's all I know how to do. I won't give up my identity without a fight."

Laure could feel Sinjin's fire. How long had it been since she'd felt the same spirit burning inside her? "I wish I had your passion."

"You do."

"I did once. It's gone now."

Sinjin sat up straighter. "Don't tell me you're thinking about retiring."

"I'm no longer thinking. I've already made the decision. This is my last year on tour. You may have thought I was joking when I said I should trade tennis for winemaking, but I was serious."

"But you're still in the top ten. You're number seven in the world. Why would you retire now?"

Sinjin sounded incredulous that Laure would walk away from the game when she was still so close to the top, but she had reached the end of her string.

"I'm twenty-seven years old. Twenty-seven used to be the prime of a tennis player's life. Now it's the time to start thinking about life after your playing days are over. There's only one way for me to go from here and that's down. The game's getting faster. The players are getting bigger. I'm never going to be any taller than five-eight. It's harder for me to generate power than it is for you Amazons."

"Have you told anyone?"

"Just you and my parents. I don't plan on saying anything to anyone else until after I've played my last match. It's going to be so hard knowing every time I walk into an arena could be the last time I play there. I don't want the extra pressure of everyone else knowing it, too."

Sinjin seemed more upset by the prospect of Laure's retirement than she did. She wasn't surprised. Sinjin was the most competitive person she had ever met. She hated to lose at anything, whether on or off the court.

"Why now?" Sinjin asked.

"I've won three Grand Slam singles titles, I've been ranked number one, and I've made more money than I could ever hope to spend. What's left for me to do?"

"Win the French Open?"

"Like that's ever going to happen."

Each May meant agony for Laure as she struggled to win matches at the only Grand Slam event she had never claimed. Her career-best finish at her country's national championship was a semifinal when she was nineteen. She had lost to eventual champion Justine Henin, the diminutive player who won the title four times in a five-year span. Laure hadn't been past the third round since that memorable run, succumbing time and time again to the pressure of playing in front of her hometown crowd.

She had finished the previous year as the fifth-ranked woman, but her ranking had recently dropped two spots as she wavered between being satisfied with her career and hungering for more. Her breaks from the tour were becoming longer and more frequent as she began to devote more of her time to the property she owned in Saint Tropez. When she wasn't maintaining her vineyard, she was using its bounty to add more bottles to her extensive wine collection.

"When your avocation gives you more satisfaction than your vocation, that's a telltale sign it's time to exit stage left."

Sinjin fingered the stylized fleur de lis on the bottle of Beaujolais. "In one way or another, we're all chasing perfection. Most of us never achieve it, especially in sports." She sounded uncharacteristically introspective. Then again, she'd had plenty of time to think. "There are worse things you could do than spend your life trying to make the perfect bottle of wine. If you need help stomping grapes or taste testing the finished results, you know where to find me."

"I might take you up on that."

Laure tried to imagine harvesting next year's crops with Sinjin at her side. The image was almost laughable. City girl Sinjin would be bored silly on the vast pastoral estate Laure called home. In less than a day, she'd turn tail and run back to South Beach. *Play hard and party harder* was her motto for a reason.

"I can't believe you're retiring," Sinjin said. "What are you going to miss most?"

"Not the travel, that's for sure. If I never see the inside of another airport after this year, that's fine with me. I'll miss all the people I've met. All the friends I've made, present company included. Friends like you are what I'm going to have problems letting go of, not the lifestyle."

"We'll still see each other, won't we?"

"All the time," Laure said with more conviction than she felt. She had never met anyone who loved tennis as much as Sinjin did. For Laure, practicing and playing were work. For Sinjin, they were more like play. Laure hated the constant travel, but Sinjin seemed addicted to it. If her body held up, she probably wouldn't stop playing until someone pried the racquet from her cold, dead hands. When Laure put her own racquets down at the end of the year, she had no idea when or if she might pick them up again.

"I hope you're hungry. Stephanie's making her world famous paella tonight."

"World famous, huh? Sounds like I picked the perfect day to visit."

Sinjin reached for the bottle of wine. "Beaujolais goes with seafood, doesn't it?"

"Beaujolais goes with everything."

Sinjin swung her legs to the side of the bed. Laure helped her to her feet. In obvious pain, Sinjin took a cautious step forward and wrapped her arms around her neck. "I've missed you."

"Same here." Laure returned Sinjin's hug. "Hurry back, okay? The tour isn't the same without you."

"Come January, I'll be saying the same to you." Sinjin leaned on Laure for support as they slowly made their way to the dining room.

"You won't even know I'm gone."

"Bullshit. I'm going to be lost without you. The highlight of my career is winning the U.S. Open doubles title with you. You're my claim to fame."

"Do I get a medal for that?"

"More like my eternal gratitude."

"If that's the best you can do."

"Bitch." Laughing, Sinjin took a playful swat at Laure's shoulder.

"That's a sound I haven't heard in far too long," Stephanie said. "Laure, I may have to keep you around."

Laure's eyes flicked from Stephanie to Sinjin and back again. "There's nowhere else I'd rather be."

QUALIFYING

Sinjin resumed training three weeks after the procedure. Her first practice session was both exhausting and frustrating. She shanked so many balls she felt like a weekend hacker instead of a seasoned pro. But there was good news: the pain she had felt for the past eleven months was gone. Had she found salvation in time to take advantage of it or had she missed her opportunity?

"Dig, dig, dig!"

Grunting with exertion, her body bathed in sweat, Sinjin fought against the resistance band that was holding her back. The workout was sheer torture. God, how she had missed it.

The day before, Laure had won the French Open. Watching the tearful scene on television, Sinjin had sent her a congratulatory text message. Laure's response? *Now it's your turn.*

To take her turn, to claim her sport's Holy Grail and win Wimbledon in front of her countrymen, Sinjin would have to start from the bottom and work her way up. Was she up to the task?

Her trainer, clutching the ends of the giant elastic band wrapped around Sinjin's waist, hung on for dear life as Sinjin dragged her around the practice court.

"Ten more steps!" Kendall Worthington called out. "Make them count! That's it. Five, four, three, two, last one. Time!" When Kendall let go of the resistance band, she and Sinjin tumbled laughing to the ground.

Sinjin remained where she landed, her muscles and lungs burning too much to move. Kendall recovered first, then reached down and pulled Sinjin to her feet.

They had briefly been teammates at the University of Miami. Kendall had decided to put her sports fitness degree to work after graduation instead of turning pro. Now she was one of the youngest certified trainers on the circuit.

"Great workout, mate. Let's get you stretched out, then we can hit the showers."

Sinjin took note of Kendall's use of the word *we*. Not too long ago, she would have leaped at the chance to spend some quality time exploring Kendall's firm body. Now all she cared about was getting her career back on track.

She lay on her back, a position that dredged up bad memories of the week she had spent practically immobile while she waited for the PRP therapy to take effect. As Kendall did her best to push her left knee past her ear, Sinjin's hamstrings screamed in protest. Sinjin flinched involuntarily.

"Am I hurting you?" Kendall lowered Sinjin's left leg and reached for her right.

"You were never known for your gentle touch."

Kendall positioned her shoulder behind Sinjin's right knee and leaned forward. "I haven't heard you complain about my touch before, gentle or otherwise." Her voice was low and husky, her eyes heavy-lidded with desire, her mouth almost close enough to kiss.

Sinjin stared into Kendall's glittering green eyes and felt... nothing. Her libido, normally as dependable as the sun rising in the east and setting in the west, seemed to have gone dormant. Women still caught her eye, but none of them captured her interest. Not for more than a few hours at a time, anyway. Who needed happily ever after? All she wanted was a warm bed, the occasional warm body, and a spot in the top ten. Nothing else mattered.

As Kendall continued to stretch her stiff muscles, Sinjin closed her eyes and allowed her mind to wander. She drifted back to the scores of sleepless nights she had spent wondering if she would ever set foot on a tennis court again. Those dark days had taught her who her true mates were. Or should she say *mate*?

Out of all her so-called friends on tour, Laure had been the only one who had come to visit her when she was laid up. The rest had sent cards, e-mails, or text messages, but they hadn't graced her with their presence. Their efforts at offering support had felt like lip service; Laure's had felt sincere. Had she held up her end of the friendship? She hoped so. Laure deserved the best. Critics might question Laure's heart on court, but there was no questioning her heart off it. Laure was the most caring, most compassionate person she had ever met. She was also drop-dead gorgeous. And the French accent didn't hurt. Women threw themselves at Laure all the time, but until Mireille came along, it had been years since Sinjin had seen her accept any of their passes. Now Mireille was gone and Laure was back on the shelf.

Sinjin felt a flicker of desire when she imagined staring into Laure's dark brown eyes. Running her hands through Laure's short brown hair. Tracing her finger across Laure's downturned mouth. Teasing her full lips to curve into a smile. She imagined the arms wrapped around her thighs, the hands stroking her skin and kneading her muscles, were Laure's. She flinched when she remembered they weren't.

Her eyes flew open. Fuck. Where had that come from?

"Okay, okay. I get the hint." Kendall gently lowered Sinjin's legs to the ground, then pulled her to her feet.

Sinjin brushed grass off the back of her workout clothes while she tried to come to terms with her fantasy—and the very real effect it had had on her. Wherever the images had originated, she needed to banish them right away. She and Laure were friends, nothing more. Nothing and no one could get in the way of her goals. Not even Laure.

"Fancy a drink?" Kendall asked.

"I can't. I promised Stephanie I'd make dinner tonight."

"Since when do you cook?"

"Okay, maybe I promised I'd pick up chicken curry on my way home."

"That sounds more like you. Get a good night's sleep. I'll see you tomorrow, yeah?"

"I can't wait."

Sinjin headed to the showers. When she came out, she found a familiar face waiting for her in the locker room.

"Laure. What the hell are you doing here? Unless the rules have changed, top ten players don't have to play qualifying rounds."

"When you told me you were working out again, I had to see it for myself."

She eyed Laure's racquet bag. "Did you bring it?"

"Bring what?"

Sinjin pursed her lips. "Don't kid a kidder. You know what I'm talking about. Come on. Out with it."

Laure reached inside the bag and pulled out the trophy she had been awarded after winning the French Open, a smaller version of the one she had shown to her cheering countrymen after yesterday's final.

Sinjin examined the sturdy silver trophy before returning it. "I can't believe you finally did it. I'm so happy for you." She gave Laure a congratulatory hug, then held her at arm's length. She had never seen Laure look so satisfied. So at peace. "Winning becomes you." She let go and took a seat on the bench. Laure sat next to her. "Shouldn't you be posing for a photo shoot at the Eiffel Tower?"

"I'd rather help you."

"What do you mean?"

"I heard you were looking for a practice partner. I came to volunteer my services."

"Why would you do that?"

"You need to qualify and I need some practice on grass if either of us is to have a shot at winning Wimbledon. You scratch my back and I'll scratch yours."

"You'd do that for me?"

"What are friends for?"

Sinjin remained skeptical. "Not every friend would make that kind of offer."

Most players, herself included, were self-absorbed. Everything revolved around them. Their bodies. Their training. Their games. Their schedules. There was no room for anyone or anything else.

Laure offered a Gallic shrug. "I guess I'm one of a kind."

"You are that."

Sinjin wished Viktoriya had followed Laure's lead. If she had, they might not be an item, but at least they'd be on speaking terms.

"Tell me all about it. Tell me how it felt to hold that trophy over your head."

Laure opened her mouth to respond but immediately closed it again. She shook her head. "There are no words."

Sinjin wanted to feel a similar sense of achievement. She wanted to be struck dumb by her own accomplishment.

"I brought something else." Laure reached into her bag again.

"How did you get through the airport with so much hardware?"

"The security guard and I got to know each other *really* well. The wedding's next week." Laure held out her Wimbledon trophy. "This is the one you want to hold."

Sinjin longed to wrap her fingers around the Ladies' Plate, the gold and silver dish awarded to the women's singles champion. She wanted to feel the ridges and bumps of its intricate design. See her name engraved next to those of past winners. The object of her desire was inches away, but she shrank from its presence.

"I can't hold it unless I win it."

"You fondled my French Open trophy. Why can't you molest this one?"

Sinjin took a deep breath to control the sudden flood of emotions.

"You know how aspiring singers pretend their toothbrushes are microphones? When I first started playing tennis, I used to pretend one of my mum's platters was the Ladies' Plate. I'd walk around the house holding it over my head like I was circling Centre Court showing it off to the crowd. One day—I think I was about eight or nine—Mum found a keychain shaped like the Ladies' Plate in a gift shop. It was so small it fit in the palm of her hand, but she had the clerk wrap it in a huge box. When she brought it home, I ripped off the wrapping paper and dug through the packaging inside. The keychain was taped to the bottom of the box. When I finally found it, Mum said, 'This might not be the actual Ladies' Plate, but one day, you'll get to hold the real thing.' I want to hold the real thing. I want that more than anything. If you can help me do that…"

Her voice trailed off. Laure wiped away her tears. "Let's get to work."

When she had first joined the tour, Sinjin had been too much of a know-it-all to accept anyone's offer of help, let alone request it. She gladly acquiesced now.

"When do we start?"

❖

Sinjin walked behind a roller hopper, gathering the dozens of tennis balls scattered around the court. The machine, which could pick up and store up to a hundred balls, bore an uncanny resemblance to a manual lawn mower.

"If tennis doesn't work out for me," she said, "I could always find work as a landscape artist."

"I have several hundred acres that need trimming," Laure said. "How much would you charge?"

"I've got to warn you. I don't come cheap." Sinjin rolled the hopper to the service line and set it up. She spread the handles, flipped the hopper upside down, and opened the lid. She took out a handful of balls and shoved them in the pockets of her tennis shorts. "Would you like me to show you how to earn some free points on your serve?"

"What's wrong with my serve?" Laure asked defensively.

"Nothing. Your percentage is always high and your placement's so good I could probably drop a grain of rice in the service box and you'd be able to hit it."

"But?"

"But you rarely break triple digits on the speed gun. If you add five, ten more miles per hour to your serve, you could make life a whole lot easier for yourself."

"Thanks, but I doubt you'd be able to turn me into an ace machine overnight."

"Just trust me, okay? The secret to a fast serve is in the service motion itself. Whether you use John McEnroe's pendulum swing or the abbreviated motion Andre Agassi used for a while, the power comes when you snap your wrist after making contact with the ball."

Sinjin took two balls out of her pocket.

"In this drill, I want you to stand behind the service line and—"

"The service line? Don't you mean the baseline? If I serve from here, I'll hit it a mile long."

"Not if you snap it down. Let me show you."

She tossed a ball in the air and raised her racquet. She hit the ball just as it reached its apex. Even at half speed, the ball rocketed across the net. Instead of flying long, it landed in the opposite service box.

Laure instantly changed from doubting to believing.

"Wow. Show me again."

Sinjin demonstrated the technique a few more times then tossed Laure a ball. "Your turn."

Laure took her position behind the service line. Sinjin talked her through the drill. Laure followed her instructions—and hit the ball straight into the ground.

"Too much snap?" she asked, turning crimson with embarrassment.

Sinjin tried not to laugh. "Here. Let me show you." Sinjin dropped her racquet and stepped forward. She curled her arm around Laure's waist and pulled her closer. She placed her hand on Laure's racquet hand and guided her through the motion.

"Toss the ball up, go after it, then snap it down."

Sinjin felt like Laure's body was an extension of her own. Together, they moved as one. The ball landed just long.

"Getting better," Laure said.

"One more time."

Sinjin's hand slid across Laure's flat stomach as she reached for another ball. She molded her body to Laure's. As they moved through the drill again, her dormant libido flared to life. She squeezed

Laure's hip, holding her tight against her. Her other hand caressed Laure's forearm before closing around her wrist. She buried her nose in Laure's hair, which was dripping with perspiration but smelled faintly of the mango-scented shampoo she favored.

"Toss the ball up."

Her nipples hardened as they pressed against Laure's back.

"Go after it."

Laure raised the racquet. Sinjin felt herself grow wet.

"Snap it down."

She wanted to lay Laure down and quickly undress her. Make love to her here on the lush grass court regardless of who was watching.

"We did it."

Laure's excited shout snapped Sinjin out of her reverie. She took a step back to give herself the distance she needed to clear her head. Laure wasn't one of her random hook-ups. How could she forget that, even for an instant?

"Let's see if you can do it on your own."

On her third attempt, Laure was able to complete the drill unassisted. She went through half the bucket of balls, missing her aim only twice. "I want to try it from the baseline. Grab the speed gun."

Sinjin pointed the handheld machine in Laure's direction. "Don't overdo it or you'll strain your wrist."

Laure went through her normal service motion. When her racquet made contact with the ball, she employed the technique Sinjin taught her. Sinjin turned the speed gun around to see the display.

"What does it say?"

Grinning, Sinjin showed her the readout.

"One twenty? That's five miles per hour over my personal best."

"I told you."

Laure gave her a high five. "Forget landscaping. Stick to tennis. You're better at it."

Sinjin felt it again. The pulsing, electric current of attraction. Laure was the unlikely source. A familiar itch began to form. One she knew from experience wouldn't be ignored for long.

❖

In Paris, Laure hadn't felt her game start to click until she reached the quarterfinals. After each training session with Sinjin, her confidence grew even higher. She knew she was playing well. She had won the French Open, after all. Was she playing well enough to win Wimbledon, too? She thought she was. Unless Sinjin played at the same level at Wimbledon as she did in practice.

The ball was flying off Sinjin's racquet. Her serve had never been bigger. Her ground strokes had never been harder. The time off had done her good. Could her still-healing body endure the stress she was subjecting it to? She was pushing herself so hard she could derail her comeback before it began.

After they split practice sets, Kendall led them through footwork drills. She stretched a rope ladder on the ground to test their lateral movement.

They concentrated on a different discipline in each training session, varying the order of the drills so they wouldn't get stale.

Movement, footwork, ground strokes, serve, volleys. The five things they would need to do well at Wimbledon. Laure's coach Nicolas Almaric, yelling instructions from the sidelines, repeated the words so often they became a mantra. Add some incense and a gong and they could have been a Buddhist chant.

Laure's hip flexors screamed as she quickly placed her feet in the spaces between each of the speed ladder's rungs. Once she finished, she waited for Sinjin to take her turn. Sinjin's face was a mask of concentration as she tried to fit her oversized feet in the tiny grids without falling on her face.

"I've got an idea," Laure said, running through the drill again.

"Should I be worried, afraid, or both?"

"Neither. Why don't we take tomorrow off? We could spend some time exploring something other than this patch of green we've been running around on for the past week. There's an exhibit at the National Gallery I've been dying to see. What do you say?"

"Would it be good for my tennis?"

"Your tennis? Probably not. Your personal edification? Definitely." She tried to counter the skeptical expression on Sinjin's face. "Tennis is a big part of my life, but I don't let it consume me. I have other interests. If I wake up and feel like I'd rather spend the day doing something other than chasing after a fuzzy yellow ball, I do. I know coming back is important to you, but you need to find a balance."

Sinjin groaned when Kendall told them to run the movement drill backward. "No offense, Laure, but I'd rather have my eyes pecked out by a flock of disease-ridden pigeons than spend a beautiful summer afternoon trapped inside a museum."

"Oh, how could I possibly take offense at that?"

Sinjin unleashed a throaty laugh, then tripped on the last rung. Laure caught her as she fell but couldn't hold her up. She grunted when she hit the ground. She grunted even louder when Sinjin landed on top of her.

Sinjin rolled over and brushed Laure's hair out of her eyes. "Are you okay? Did I hurt you?"

Laure wrapped her arms around her middle. "Just a few broken ribs. Maybe a fractured vertebra or two. Wait. I forgot about the ruptured spleen." She let out a melodramatic howl of pain.

Sinjin's eyes filled with concern that slowly evolved into mirth. "Damn. You almost had me."

"Almost doesn't count."

Kendall and Nicolas leaned over them to make sure they were unhurt. "Okay," Nicolas said, clapping his hands. "That's enough for today. Let's quit while we're ahead."

Kendall rolled up the ladder and tossed it over her shoulder. "Same time tomorrow, ladies."

"Thanks for the warning." Sinjin lay on her side. She plucked a blade of grass and slowly trailed it across Laure's cheek. "Have I told you how much I appreciate you being here?"

"Several hundred times, yes."

"You should come out with us tonight."

"Us?"

"Abby's in town for qualifying. I owe her and Kendall rain checks for drinks. I figured I'd kill two birds with one stone. And perhaps scratch an itch or two in the process."

Laure brushed Sinjin's hand away and abruptly sat up to hide her irritation.

She and Sinjin had been working side-by-side for days. Sweating. Straining. Trying to improve their bodies and lift their games. She felt closer to her than she ever had before. Closer to her than she'd ever felt with anyone. Were her feelings of friendship slowly being replaced by something much deeper?

When had it happened? Was it the day she'd arrived when Sinjin had told her that incredibly sweet story about her mother buying her a keychain shaped like the Ladies' Plate? Or was it even earlier than that? When she'd seen Sinjin so vulnerable after the procedure on her knees? Was it after her breakup with Mireille when Sinjin's endless stream of bad jokes had helped ease the pain? Or was it three years ago when, after the U.S. Open doubles final, Sinjin had given her a kiss to which none she had received before or since could compare?

"I'll tell Mother Superior you won't be needing that room after all."

"Definitely not. My dry spell's over. Or it will be in a couple of hours. Right on time, too. For a while there, my sex drive was practically nonexistent. Since we started working out, though, I've been back in tune. You should come with us tonight. Wouldn't you rather spend your free time in a bar filled with hot women than in a musty museum?"

Laure tossed Sinjin's earlier question back at her. "Would it be good for my tennis?"

Sinjin smiled. "Your tennis? No. Your sex life? Definitely."

"No offense, Sinjin, but I'd rather have my fingernails ripped out one by one than sleep with someone I just met."

Sinjin's smile faded. "Oh, how could I possibly take offense to that?" She pushed herself to her feet. "We've had this argument before, you know."

"Not argument. Discussion."

"Argument. Discussion. Whatever you want to call it." Sinjin drank deeply from a bottle of water. "I like quantity. You prefer quality. I'm not going to change and neither are you."

"I'm not asking you to change. I'm just trying to understand the one thing about you that's always puzzled me." Laure poured water over her head to cool off. "What is it about the thrill of the hunt that excites you so much? Why can't you find what you're looking for in one woman instead of several?"

"Because Miss Right expects me to take out the trash and tell her if her arse looks fat in her favorite pair of jeans. Miss Right Now doesn't expect anything from me except a couple of laughs and a few multiple orgasms. Which relationship sounds more appealing, the one that requires heavy lifting or the one that offers the path of least resistance?"

"The one formed with someone who knows me inside and out. Who cares about me for who I am and loves me despite my faults."

"When you put it that way, I look like a proper arsehole," Sinjin said with a grin. "If you'll excuse me, I'm going to drown my sorrows in a pint of Newcastle and find a nice, soft shoulder to lean on while I cry."

Laure watched her go. "Good luck on both counts."

Sinjin slowly slid a fingertip between Abby's shoulder blades. Her tongue circled a pale pink nipple. Abby shuddered in her arms.

"Whatever you do," Abby said, riding her fingers, "please don't stop."

"I don't intend to."

When Abby came, her keening cries were like music to Sinjin's ears. A song she hadn't heard in far too long. But something was off. The music was flat. The melody wasn't as she remembered it. Instead of a symphony, she was treated to Muzak.

She reached for her clothes. Sex with Abby had been fun but unfulfilling. It had taken the edge off, but it hadn't satisfied. She couldn't get away fast enough.

Abby sat up. The sheet slid down her alabaster skin. "Where are you going?"

"There's someplace I have to be."

"Now? I was gearing up for round two."

Sinjin gave her a peck on the lips. "Rain check."

"This *was* your bloody rain check."

"I need another one."

Abby held Sinjin's face in her hands and gave her a lingering kiss. "Are you sure you can't stay?"

Sinjin covered Abby's exposed breasts. "I'm sure."

She made a quick pit stop, then took the train to Notting Hill, the west London neighborhood that would serve as Laure's base of operations for the next three weeks.

When Laure opened the door, she was wearing a pair of running shorts and a T-shirt that featured a parody of Edvard Munch's *Scream*. The famous figure from Munch's painting had been replaced by Homer Simpson. "Did you scratch your itch?" Laure asked, closing the door behind her.

"Yes. Thank you for asking."

"That didn't take long."

Laure took a seat on the couch. Sinjin joined her.

"It doesn't take long if you know what you're doing."

"Then I must be doing something wrong." Laure flashed her wry sense of humor. "No, that's impossible. I'm French. No matter what the Italians say, we invented romance."

"Not so fast. I've had sex with plenty of French girls who had no idea what they were doing."

"You should try making love with a French woman instead."

"I could take that several ways, you know."

"Why don't you settle for one?"

Sinjin was in her comfort zone. She could flirt with a beautiful woman with her eyes closed. But this wasn't just any beautiful woman. This was Laure. Someone who knew her better than anyone else. Someone who saw past her jokey exterior to the bundle of insecurities that lay beneath. Someone who got her in every sense of the word.

She flashed back to the conversation they'd had in Roehampton. When Laure had listed the qualities she sought in Miss Right, she had said she was looking for someone who knew her inside and out. Who loved her for who she was, despite her faults.

Am I looking for the same thing?

Why had it taken her so long to think of Laure as anything other than a friend when she obviously had the potential to be so much more?

Maybe I've been looking in the wrong places.

"Do you have a woman in mind for me?"

"I'm horrible at matchmaking. I'll let you make up your own mind."

Sinjin smiled at the give and take. She couldn't tell which was more exciting, the fact that Laure was flirting with her or the fact that she was doing it so subtly. She reached for the bottle of wine she had picked up on her way from Abby's hotel. "I bought this, but I'm not sure if it's any good. Can you help me out?"

Laure grabbed the bottle and turned it around to see the label. She rolled her eyes when she realized the bottle was one of hers. She tapped her finger against the fleur de lis on the label. "This vintner has a pretty good reputation." She found a corkscrew in the kitchen and inserted it into the bottle.

"A reputation doesn't mean anything," Sinjin said as Laure expertly removed the cork. "It's just something to be lived up or down to. I'm not as bad as mine. I'd love to know if you're as good as yours."

"There's only one way to find out." Laure poured two glasses and offered Sinjin one. "Try me and see."

"We're not still talking about wine, are we?"

Laure raised her glass to her lips. "Were we ever?"

❖

Movement, footwork, ground strokes, serve, volleys.

Sinjin repeated the words to herself as she sat in her chair after the ten-minute warm-up. It had come down to this. She was about to play Austrian journeywoman Emme Wechselberger in the final round of qualifying. If she won the match, she would achieve her goal: to make it into the main draw at Wimbledon. She didn't care if she would have to play the top seed, the defending champion, or another qualifier in the first round. She just wanted to get there. She couldn't win the tournament if she wasn't in the field. And she couldn't make it into the field without her friends and family cheering her on.

She located Stephanie, Kendall, and Laure in the stands. Her sister, her trainer, and her best friend. Three women she'd be lost without. Stephanie, who had guided and cared for her for years. Kendall, who pushed her to her limits and past them. Laure, whose role in her life was once well-defined but had recently gone blurry around the edges.

Laure cupped her hands around her mouth. "Let's go, Sin!"

Sinjin tapped her racquet against the court for luck the way she always did before a big match. She didn't think she'd need luck. In fact, she felt absurdly confident. She was paired against a player to whom she had never lost.

Emme was a consistent but pedestrian baseliner. Lacking a big weapon she could use to hurt her opponents, she had never risen higher than ninety-seven in the world. Her current ranking was nearly twice that number. She and Abby McGuinness had reached the U.S. Open doubles final, but she hadn't come close to repeating the accomplishment in the three years since. She had reached the final round of singles qualifying at Roehampton via walkover in the first round when her opponent had not been able to take the court because of an ankle injury sustained in practice. She had outlasted her second-round opponent, winning a compelling but error-filled match in three long sets. At thirty-six years old and nearing the end of her career, she was given little chance of upsetting Sinjin. Most expected her to be nothing more than the answer to the trivia question, "Who did Sinjin Smythe defeat in order to reach her ninth Wimbledon?"

Someone forgot to tell Emme.

She came out firing. Sinjin rushed the net at every available opportunity only to be met with stinging passing shots aimed at her feet. She made some amazing half-volleys to stay in the set, but facing break point at 5-4 down, she pushed a forehand volley wide to lose the set 6-4.

The crowd gasped, then lapsed into stunned silence. Furious with herself, Sinjin stalked to the sidelines and sat in her chair. She had underestimated her opponent, an error even more critical than the unforced one she had made on the previous point.

In the stands, Laure, Kendall, and Stephanie looked anxious.

"I'm okay," Sinjin mouthed, trying to allay their fears.

She bounced back to win the second set 6-1, a breadstick in tennis parlance. She lost just two points in her first four service games in the third set but couldn't manufacture a break. With the score knotted at four-all, she won the first two points on Emme's serve. If she took the next two, she could serve out the match and secure the last spot in the Wimbledon field.

The contest was the last singles match of the day. Some of the players who had competed in and won earlier matches had stuck around to show their support. Some were seated in the stands; most stood in the entrance of the tunnel that led to the locker room. Rejuvenated by the results of the PRP procedure—and Laure's win in Paris—Sinjin had put off thoughts of retirement, but her friends on tour seemed to sense her window of opportunity was closing. They shouted encouragement as she prepared to receive serve.

At 0-30, Emme surprised her by pumping in a big serve and following it to the net. She volleyed the high return into the open court to close the gap to 15-30. She earned the next point with a beautiful topspin lob that barely cleared Sinjin's outstretched racquet and dropped in the corner.

Sinjin was still two points from the game, but 30-all felt a lot different than 0-30. On the next point, she sliced a backhand down the middle of the court and followed it to the net. She hit what seemed like a perfect approach shot, but Emme managed to steer her passing shot down the line for a winner.

"Come on!" the usually stoic Emme yelled, pumping herself up.

Sinjin tried to remain calm, but overanxious, she smothered a forehand and deposited it in the middle of the net. Instead of serving for the match, she would be serving to stay in it.

As she sat in her chair during the changeover, she bounced her legs to keep them loose. She didn't feel nervous. Her adrenaline was pumping too hard for that. She tried not to dwell on the missed opportunities in the previous game. There would be plenty of time for reflection later. She needed to focus on the task at hand: getting to five-all.

On the first point, she uncorked her biggest serve of the day, a 122-mph screamer down the middle, for her fourteenth ace. Emme responded on the next point, however. Utilizing the tactics that had worked so well in the first set, she blasted a return at Sinjin's feet. Sinjin couldn't dig out the half-volley and lost the point to level the score at 15-all.

Sinjin bounced on the balls of her feet to remind herself to stay on her toes. Three points from losing, she couldn't afford to get caught flat-footed. She threw in an off-speed serve hoping to catch Emme by surprise, but Emme jumped all over it to take a 15-30 lead.

Just bring the heat, dammit! If she can take it, shake her hand and go home.

She hit a hard, flat serve that crowded in close to Emme's body.

Emme tried to move out of the way. Unable to extend her arms to generate power, she choked up on her racquet and muscled a backhand return. The ball hit the top of the net, dribbled over to Sinjin's side, and rolled to a stop for double match point.

Sometimes it was better to be lucky than good.

Emme held up one hand in mock apology and walked to the other side of the court to receive serve.

Shaking her head in disbelief, Sinjin tried to maintain her concentration. She needed to win the next four points to stay in the match. Her fifteenth ace brought the score to 30-40 and the crowd to its feet.

"One more!" someone shouted. "One more!"

Sinjin loved and hated playing in England. When things were going well, she fed off the energy of the fans. When things got tough, though, the fans' apprehension seeped into her. "Believe in yourself," she whispered, trying to hold her uncertainty at bay.

Serving to the ad court, she second-guessed herself. Instead of going with her kick serve to Emme's backhand, she went for the big one down the middle. Emme jumped on the forehand return and, anticipating a weak response, followed her shot to the net.

Knowing Emme's net play was the weakest part of her game, Sinjin didn't aim for the lines. She went right at her, expecting Emme to miss the volley. She planted her feet and hit a forehand as hard as she could.

Emme stuck her racquet out, then, apparently sensing the ball wasn't hit with enough topspin to keep it in the court, she tried to jerk the racquet out of the way. She didn't move quite fast enough. The ball ticked off her frame and landed six inches beyond the baseline.

The linesperson called the ball out, but because Emme had touched the ball while it was in flight, Sinjin should have been awarded the point.

Sinjin pumped her fists and turned to head to the baseline to serve at deuce when the chair umpire said, "Game, set, match, Miss Wechselberger."

Everything happened at once.

Emme thrust her arms in the air and ran to the net for the post-match handshake. The knowledgeable crowd, aware that the point should have been awarded to Sinjin, loudly voiced its disapproval.

"No!" Sinjin ran to the umpire's chair, pointing to her ear and to Emme's racquet. "The ball hit her frame. Didn't you hear that?" When the chair umpire shook his head, Sinjin turned to Emme for confirmation. "Didn't you get a piece of that shot?"

Emme shrugged and pleaded ignorance. "I didn't feel anything."

Sinjin gaped at her in open-mouthed shock. Tennis, like golf, was a gentleman's game. One in which players were supposed to call infractions on themselves if they knew they had broken a rule. By not owning up to what had just happened, Emme had violated one of the unwritten rules of the sport.

The crowd booed lustily as Emme quickly packed her bags and retreated to the locker room.

Unwilling to leave the court, Sinjin sat in her chair and buried her face in a towel. When she looked up, her eyes were wet. Stephanie was crying, too, but Sinjin noticed Laure was trying to put on a brave face.

"I'm proud of you." Laure rose with the rest of the crowd to give Sinjin a standing ovation.

Walking with her head down, Sinjin acknowledged the cheers as she headed disconsolately to the locker room. A cordon of players greeted her as she entered the tunnel. Each offered words of encouragement or a pat on the back.

"Tough luck."

"Bad break."

"Good fight out there."

Overwhelmed, Sinjin nodded her thanks but kept trudging along. Emme, already showered and dressed, was waiting for her in the locker room.

"I'm sorry, but I had to do it. You're young. You'll have many more chances to make Wimbledon, but this was my last one."

Sinjin cast a wary glance at Anke Schroeder, the only other person in the room. The eighteen-year-old junior phenom from Munich was being touted as the next Steffi Graf. One of the day's winners, the pony-tailed blonde would be making her Wimbledon debut in a few days. Though single-minded on court, Anke was still wide-eyed off it. Sinjin didn't want to lose her temper in front of someone who was still so impressionable.

"You know what?" Sinjin fought to keep her voice level. "I'm not mad at you for what you did. I'm mad at myself for putting myself in the position in the first place. You did what you felt you had to do. If you can live with it, so can I. Just don't ask me to respect you in the morning."

Emme trudged out of the room and Sinjin headed to the showers, where she finally let her emotions hold sway. When she returned to the locker room, Anke was still sitting in the same spot.

"Did you forget your way home?"

"I've been thinking." Anke's expression was dour.

"Was it painful for you?" Sinjin asked, trying to get Anke to lighten up.

Anke was a stern taskmaster, which caused her to expect more from her game than it was ready to give. She wouldn't get the results she wanted until she learned to relax. Those pesky comparisons to Steffi Graf didn't help. But the comparisons weren't going to go away any time soon. Germany's rabid sports fans were eager to find the next Steffi. The next Boris Becker. But Sinjin knew players like those two all-time greats came along only once in a lifetime. Anke would have to "settle" for being herself. If she could convince her compatriots to do the same thing, she would sleep a lot better at night.

"It doesn't feel right that I should qualify for Wimbledon and you don't. You deserve it as much as I do."

Sinjin sat next to Anke on the long pine bench that divided the room in half. "How many matches did I win this week?"

"Two."

"How many did you win?"

"Three."

"Then who deserves to qualify?"

"But you got cheated."

"Out of one point, not the whole match."

"You were my idol growing up." Anke's comment made Sinjin feel honored and ancient at the same time. "I want to see you win Wimbledon one day."

"So do I." Sinjin had learned some important lessons from the loss—what not to do during a pressure situation and how to keep her head when everything seemed to be going against her. She had also learned her body could hold up during a long match. She hadn't thought about her knees even once during the heated contest. She longed to be able to put what she had learned to use. "It's not too late. As the highest seed to lose today, I can still get in if someone pulls out."

Speculation was running rampant that a strained wrist might keep two-time defending champion Blake Freeman from playing at

Wimbledon. She was expected to play a couple exhibition matches to test the wrist, then announce her decision on the Friday before the tournament started. Injured or not, Sinjin couldn't imagine Blake pulling out of the event. No woman had won three consecutive Wimbledon singles titles since Steffi Graf in the early '90s. With her eye on the history books, Blake would probably play even if her wrist was in a cast.

"I'll see you next week," Sinjin assured Anke. But as she gathered her belongings, she didn't plan on waiting by the phone.

Laure, Stephanie, and Kendall were waiting for her outside the locker room. She had expected to be greeted by a sea of long faces, but Laure was positively beaming.

"You got in."

Sinjin was stunned. "Did Blake pull out?"

"No, but Catarina Sundstrom did." Laure scrolled through the Web page displayed on her BlackBerry. "She ate some bad pizza after the French Open final and came down with food poisoning."

Catarina had lost the final to Laure in three epic sets, winning the first set 6-3 before falling 8-6 in the third.

"Serves her right," Stephanie said. "Who goes to a gastronomic capital like Paris and orders pizza?"

Sinjin sagged with relief. All the hard work she thought had gone to waste still had a chance to pay dividends. "I'm starving. What's for dinner?"

"Definitely not pizza, that's for sure."

Stephanie and Kendall begged off dinner—Stephanie had to put the finishing touches on the design for her latest window installation and Kendall wanted to hit the bars—so Sinjin and Laure headed to the house Laure had rented in Notting Hill.

"Now that you've made the tournament, what are your goals?" Laure asked over steaming plates of takeout Pad Thai.

"Win at least one round. If I do that, I want to make it to the third round, which is something I've never done. If I do that, my goal would be to make it to the second week. If I could sneak into the quarterfinals somehow, it would earn me membership in the Last Eight Club." Membership in the exclusive society was limited solely to players who had reached the quarterfinals or better at Wimbledon. "That would be something to write home about."

Laure snared some green papaya salad with her chopsticks. "My goals are a little different. I brought an evening gown with me because I'm planning on attending the Champions Ball. If you play your cards right, you could come with me. Either as my date or the champion."

The black-tie affair was held on Wimbledon's final day. The guests of honor were the players who had won the singles, doubles, and mixed doubles crowns. It used to be required for the singles winners to share a dance until, much to the players' delight, the quaint tradition was discontinued. Now they posed with their hard-earned trophies instead.

"I thought you were retiring. I thought your passion was gone."

"Believe me, it's back. You helped put it there."

"Me? What did I do?"

"You fought your heart out to get back on court. Then you fought even harder to stay there. If that isn't inspiring, I don't know what is."

"Does this mean you're not still planning to retire at the end of the year?"

"No. I'm still walking away after the year-end championships, but I want to go out in style. It's been almost ten years since a woman won the French Open and Wimbledon in the same year. I'd love to accomplish the feat."

If Sinjin won, the victory would be even more historic. No British woman had won Wimbledon in over thirty years. The drought for British men was twice as long.

Sinjin was aware of the seemingly insurmountable odds she faced. A couple unseeded men—all-time greats Boris Becker and Goran Ivanisevic—had aced their way to the Wimbledon title, but no woman seeded lower than thirteen had ever performed the same feat. And the woman who had pulled off that miracle was Venus Williams when she had found her game at the right time and raced to her fourth title. To join their ranks, Sinjin would have to play like she had her first year on tour, when her best years were ahead of her and not behind her. She would have to play better than she ever had and do it not once but seven times. With fresh legs and rusty ground strokes.

As she rode the train back to Soho, she issued herself a challenge.

You didn't turn pro to make the second week of Wimbledon. You turned pro to win the whole damn thing. So go out there and prove to yourself and everyone else that you can do it. No matter who's standing in your way.

FIRST ROUND

L aure stared at the draw sheet. Most players didn't want to look too far ahead—you couldn't play everyone in the field, and you could psych yourself out if you spent too much time plotting out potential matchups—but she wanted to see where the top players fell so she could know which ones she would have to worry about. Though the tennis gods had cut Laure a break, they hadn't granted Sinjin any favors. There were a couple of potential matchups in the second week that could give Laure cause for concern, but the first week's matches should prove no more strenuous than a practice session. Sinjin's road to the final, however, was littered with land mines.

Although she had inherited Catarina Sundstrom's spot, Sinjin hadn't been given her draw, which would have matched her against another qualifier in the first round. Instead, she would face the eighth seed—former French Open champion Rosana de los Santos. Rosana was better on clay than on grass, but she had consistent results on every surface and had made at least the quarterfinals of ten straight tournaments. Beating her would take a monumental effort, but if Sinjin was up to the challenge, a chance for revenge lurked in the second round. If Emme won her opening-round match and Sinjin upset Rosana, they would square off once the women's field was winnowed to sixty-four.

Besides Rosana and Emme, Sinjin faced a potential quarterfinal clash with second seed Blake Freeman and a semifinal against Blake's third-seeded sister Chandler. Talk about your rough draws.

Between them, the Freeman sisters had appeared in nine of the last ten Wimbledon finals, taking the trophy back to the sprawling Manhattan apartment they shared on seven occasions. Blake had won the title four times to Chandler's three. Chandler was eager to catch up to and pass her big sister. She was widely considered to be the better player, but her acting aspirations often drew her attention away from her tennis.

A would-be movie star, she had missed most of the run-up to the clay court season in order to take part in a publicity tour for her latest film. The London release of the movie was timed to coincide with the start of Wimbledon. When most players would be anxiously anticipating their first matches, Chandler would be walking the red carpet.

Blake's interests were as wide-ranging as her sister's, but at twenty-seven, she had rededicated herself to tennis in order to capitalize on the remaining three years she intended to play. If Viktoriya lost before the final and Blake went on to win the tournament, Blake would reclaim the number one ranking she hadn't held in five years.

The bottom half of the draw, where Laure resided, wasn't nearly as loaded as the top half, but the player who made her way out of it wouldn't have it easy. Viktoriya Vasilyeva, Serena Williams, and Maria Sharapova all loomed as potential roadblocks. Most experts were picking Viktoriya to make the final. She had been gifted a cupcake draw, and the week before, she had shaken off a mid-season slump to win the warm-up tournament in Birmingham. If she held her nerve—and her serve—Queen Viktoriya could prolong her reign.

Not if Laure had anything to say about it. She wanted to be the one who advanced out of the bottom section, putting an end to Viktoriya's hot streak and her era of domination on the way. Nothing short of winning the tournament would give her greater pleasure.

She opened two bottles of red wine so they could breathe. She had invited a few friends over for a small pre-tournament dinner party so she could salvage a bit of sanity before the madness began. Nicolas arrived first. She immediately put him to work lighting the lanterns that lined the patio.

She headed to the kitchen to check on the ratatouille, a hearty vegetable stew that contained eggplant, zucchini, green peppers, onions, garlic, and tomatoes. She had been cooking for less than thirty minutes, but the way the flavors had blended, the results tasted like she had been slaving over the stove for hours.

"Perfect."

She lowered the flame on the burner and raised the volume on the TV when the talking heads on the Wimbledon preview show playing in the background piped up.

"What do you think of Sinjin Smythe's chances at this year's tournament?" one asked.

"We'd be better served pinning our hopes for a women's champion on young Clair Wilkinson," his partner replied. "She won the Wimbledon junior championship two years ago at the ripe old age of fourteen and has shown tremendous promise in her first full year as a pro. Her ranking is high enough that she made it into the main draw this year without benefit of a wild card. The same cannot be said for Sinjin Smythe, who barely made the tournament this year and is in danger of becoming a footnote. She is a lucky loser who lost in the last round of qualifying and got in the main draw only because another player was taken ill. She has the game to make a run, but I question her nerves. They've betrayed her in the past and I don't see why this year should be any different. Plus, she's working without a full-time coach, which never helps. She's hired Andrew Grey on a part-time basis, but he's been out of the game so long I fear it might have passed him by. It would make a good story if Sinjin were to do well here, but I just don't see it happening. I'd bet my house she won't even make it out of the first round, let alone advance to the second week."

Laure aimed the remote control at the television and turned it off. "I'll take that bet."

❖

Sinjin checked her watch and groaned in frustration. She picked up her mobile. Her call went directly to voice mail. "Steph, it's me.

You were supposed to be here fifteen minutes ago. There are four hungry people waiting for you, so if you know what's good for you, you'll get your arse home and—"

"Oi, watch the language! I thought I taught you better than that." Two bulky boxes balanced precariously in her arms, Stephanie kicked the front door closed with the side of one Manolo Blahnik-clad foot.

Sinjin rushed to relieve Stephanie of her burden. "Where shall I put these?"

Stephanie pointed to the coffee table. "There's fine."

Sinjin fingered the packing tape on one of the boxes. "What's all this?"

"Open it and find out."

Sinjin ripped the tape off one of the boxes and cautiously opened the flaps. She pulled out a set of tennis whites that, despite the high-tech fibers they were made of, looked like they belonged in an archival photo from the 1920s. Anyone wearing the outfit would look right at home with a flapper on one arm and a wooden racquet draped across the other.

The cream cardigan was monogrammed with her initials—SIS—on the left breast. The white button-down shirt and white pants sported a designer label that she had never seen before.

"Are these for me?"

Stephanie pursed her MAC-covered lips. "Who else would they be for? Just because you lost your clothing contract doesn't mean you have to go on court looking like shite, so I decided to dress you myself."

Sinjin slipped her arms through one of the sweaters. Stephanie narrowed her eyes as she checked the fit.

"I only commissioned four outfits. Not because I don't think you can win more than four matches but because I didn't have time to pull together an order larger than that. There are two pairs of pants and two pairs of shorts. If it's hot, you can go with the shorts. If it's cooler or if it rains, you can go with the pants so you can keep your legs warm. The material's pretty forgiving in both so you should be able to get down for the low volleys without feeling restricted in any way. You know how they say it's better to look good than to feel good? Well, you're going to look great and play even better."

Sinjin laid a hand on Stephanie's arm. "You feel it, too?"

"With every fiber of my being. This fortnight's going to be special. I'm just glad I can be a part of it."

Sinjin gave her a hug and rushed to the bedroom to try on the clothes. She examined her reflection in the full-length mirror. Her new gear fit her perfectly. The sweater clung to her broad shoulders and hugged her waist. The pants were loose enough to allow freedom of movement but form-fitting enough to avoid being a hindrance when she played. The cream and white materials perfectly complemented her light brown skin.

In the living room, she turned in a slow circle then paused for inspection. "How do I look?"

Stephanie beamed with pride. "Like a future Wimbledon champion."

❖

Laure dipped a wooden spoon into the bubbling stew. She blew on the sample and held it out to Sinjin. "Taste this and tell me if it needs anything."

Sinjin sampled the offering. "What it needs is to be put in a bowl and served immediately."

Laure smiled and turned off the burner. Sinjin handed her six heavy earthenware bowls. Laure carefully ladled some of the stew into each bowl and laid a thick piece of toasted French bread on top. "Are you ready for this?"

"You bet." Sinjin's stomach growled in obvious anticipation.

"Not this," Laure said, indicating the food. "That." She jerked her chin toward the newspaper on the counter. The sports section featured wall-to-wall Wimbledon coverage and the tournament hadn't even begun.

"I'll never be ready for that, but I am ready to play. I wish I were playing tomorrow so I could burn off some of my nervous energy, but I'm not on the schedule until Tuesday." Sinjin helped Laure place the bowls on a serving tray. "What about you?"

"I'm playing tomorrow. First match on Court One."

Because they were on opposite sides of the draw, their timetables would be reversed. When Laure was scheduled to play, Sinjin would have the day off and vice versa. For the first week at least. If they kept winning, their schedules would begin to coincide on the second Monday of the event when all the remaining players in both the men's and women's fields would take the court.

"Viktoriya is scheduled for Centre Court. Novak Djokovic opens play because he's the defending champion, but Viktoriya will be the first woman who gets to play on Centre Court this year. I've played Wimbledon ten times, either as a junior or a pro, but I've never played a match on Centre. What's it like?"

Sinjin's voice was reverential, fitting for a discussion of the court often referred to as the cathedral of tennis.

"The sight lines are amazing. You never lose the ball in the lights or the background. The acoustics are incredible. You can hear the ball coming off your opponent's strings so you could close your eyes and still be able to tell if she has hit the ball flat or with topspin. The fans are always fair. They applaud a good shot, even if it's at the expense of one of their own."

"So if I played you, you're saying the crowd would be fifty-fifty?"

Laure grinned. "Maybe sixty-forty. But if you win, I'll buy you a bottle of champagne."

"And if you win, I'll buy you a crate of English strawberries."

"Sounds like a delicious combination."

"Too bad we can't share the title. Then we could have both."

"I wish we could. I don't want to see either of us lose. Unless it's to each other. That's the only reasonably acceptable outcome."

Sinjin didn't look convinced. "You know how this works. Only one of us can win. Whoever wants it more will walk away with the title."

"Which would you rather have, a trophy in your hands or me in your bed?"

"Why can't I have both?"

"I want this title as much as you do. I know how it feels to hold that trophy. I've only heard how good it feels to hold you."

Sinjin put her hands on Laure's waist and pulled her closer. "We can change that at any time, you know."

When Sinjin bent to kiss her, Laure placed a finger on her lips. "Let's see where this is going before we go there. Let's take it slow."

"We've known each other forever. We've been friends for years. If we move any slower, we'll be moving backward."

"Sinjin, I just got out of one relationship. Even though I'm attracted to you, I don't want to jump feet-first into another one. I want to make sure I'm more than an itch you want to scratch. I don't want to be someone you sleep with and walk away from. I don't want to have sex with you. I want to make love with you."

"You're right," Sinjin said after a long pause. "I have been doing it wrong."

❖

Sinjin trailed Rosana de los Santos onto Court Fourteen. As was her wont, Rosana claimed the seat to the chair umpire's right. Sinjin dropped her racquet bag next to the chair on the far side and pulled out the racquet she intended to use at the beginning of the match. She banged the strings against the heel of her hand to check the tension. Satisfied that the string job had not degraded overnight, she pantomimed a few practice swings and headed to the net to wait for the coin toss.

She had hoped the match would be scheduled for one of the main show courts, namely hallowed Centre Court or Court One. Instead, it was placed on Court Fourteen, the eighth largest court on the grounds, located directly beneath ESPN's broadcast studio. Sinjin could see the back of the lead anchor's well-coiffed head as he and his fellow commentators prepared to go on-air.

She searched the stands until she located her supporters. Stephanie was already gnawing on her fingernails, but Nicolas and Laure flashed her thumbs up signs. The day before, Laure had won her first round match in straight sets. Her opponent had been a wild card entrant playing only her second tour-level match. Overmatched and overwhelmed, the youngster had gone down in forty-five minutes. Sinjin would consider herself lucky if one of her sets lasted that long. The way Rosana played, they could be on court a while.

She took one last look around, then directed her focus where it belonged: on the match.

Rosana won the toss and elected to receive. Most players chose to serve first so they could jump out to an early lead before their opponents could calm their nerves. Rosanna preferred the opposite approach. She liked to go for a quick break of serve before her foe could find her rhythm. Pounding her ground strokes from the very first point, she'd take the first set before the player on the other side of the net knew what hit her.

The weather was warm—nearly eighty degrees. Despite the balmy temperatures, Sinjin had elected to wear the pants Stephanie had designed for her instead of the shorts. But she didn't want her fashion statement to be the only thing written about the next day. She intended to make a statement with her game as well.

She shed the cardigan and took a quick sip of water. The crowd, apprehensive yet hopeful, applauded both players as they headed to their respective baselines.

Sinjin accepted three balls from the ball boy and closely examined each one. She discarded the one with the most fuzz, keeping the two she thought would move through the air faster. She slipped one ball into her pocket and bounced the other one off her racquet face while Rosana waited for late-arriving spectators to take their seats.

"Seats quickly, please," the chair umpire said. "The players are ready."

The stragglers grabbed the nearest seats.

"*Gracias*," Rosana said sarcastically, showing uncharacteristic edginess.

Ask any player and she would say the most difficult matches to win were the first one and the last one. In the first round, you were nervous because you didn't have a measuring stick to judge where your game was. Sure, you might have been playing well in practice, but practice didn't count. How would you fare when the pressure was on? When losing meant going home, not scheduling another practice session. As the old saying went, you couldn't win a Grand Slam tournament in the first week; you could only lose one.

Sinjin had fallen prey to the pressure of a Grand Slam tournament before, letting the strain of it overwhelm her as she failed to fulfill the potential her coaches had spotted in her when she was a kid. When the match began, though, she put the past behind her. She played like she had nothing to lose and everything to gain. She went for her shots, hitting out on everything and carving her slice shots so finely the crowd gasped each time the ball grazed the net on its way over.

Rosana was the one who seemed to be succumbing to nerves. Normally placid on court, she barked at everyone in sight, herself included.

"Hit the ball, Rosana!" she screamed in Spanish after her tentative approach shot landed short and Sinjin's backhand flew past her for a winner.

The crowd erupted. Not because of Rosana's outburst but because Sinjin had reached set point. She had a chance to take the first set and start the second serving first—a huge psychological advantage.

Sinjin assumed her return stance and tried to determine where Rosana was going to direct her serve. Boris Becker used to unconsciously stick his tongue in the same direction he intended to place his delivery. Other players' tells were more subtle—a grip change here, a slight shift in stance there. The best servers were the best masters of disguise. The best returners were the best body language experts.

With her left hand, Rosana bounced the ball twice. Her right hand gripped her racquet as if it were a frying pan. After she adjusted her grip, she extended her index finger. The last time she did that, she hit a serve out wide to Sinjin's forehand. Cheating in that direction, Sinjin took a step to her left when Rosana tossed the ball in the air.

The serve was perfectly placed, but Sinjin was there for it. Swinging freely, she cracked a forehand and followed it to the net.

Her eyes as wide as saucers, Rosana scrambled to get to the return. Her dimpled shoes dug into the lush grass. She lunged for the ball, her racquet an extension of her arm. She flicked her wrist, intending to hit a defensive squash shot to keep herself in the point. The ball passed just out of reach.

"Game, first set, Miss Smythe," the chair umpire said.

"Yes!" Sinjin clenched her fists and sprinted to her chair, the crowd's cheers echoing in her ears.

In the stands, Laure, Stephanie, and Kendall were celebrating like the match was over, but Sinjin kept telling herself the job wasn't done. Winning the second set would be even harder than winning the first. Rosana, not wanting to be the tournament's first upset victim, wasn't going to go down without a fight. Known for her endurance, a long match was just what she wanted. Fitness wouldn't be an issue for Sinjin—she had put in too many hours training with Laure and Kendall to run out of gas during a match—but she wanted to keep things as uncomplicated as possible. She didn't want to give Rosana time to find her A-game.

She gave herself a pep talk during the changeover.

Concentrate on holding your serve and take your chances on hers when she gives them to you. The pressure's on her, not you. You're not even supposed to be here.

She lost just five points in her first five service games in the second set, but Rosana, playing the kind of attacking tennis that won her the U.S. Open two years before, was just as strong. When Sinjin held at love to go up six games to five, the set seemed destined to end in a tiebreaker.

In a tiebreaker, the rules were simple—the winner was the first player to accumulate seven points with at least a two-point advantage. With the stakes this high, though, a tiebreaker would be anything but simple. If Sinjin won, the match was over. If Rosana won, they would play a third set with a spot in Wimbledon's second round on the line.

Sinjin's career singles record was a tick above five hundred, but her tiebreak record was an eye-opening seventy-five percent. "If she could play nothing but tiebreakers, she'd be number one in the world," went the line on her in the locker room. "Otherwise, she's just another player."

Rosana—and the crowd—was waiting for Sinjin to crack. For her to realize how close she was to the biggest victory of her life and tighten up.

❖

In the stands, Laure examined Sinjin's face for signs of weakness. She saw none. In fact, she had never seen Sinjin looking so relaxed—on a tennis court, anyway. *Her* blood pressure, on the other hand, was off the charts.

"How do you stand it?" she asked Stephanie after Rosana held serve to force the tiebreaker. When she played, she had a say in the outcome. As a spectator, she was helpless. She preferred being in control. During her first round win, her nerves had disappeared as soon as she played the first point. Nearly two sets into Sinjin's match, she was a basket case.

"I used to go through a pack of cigarettes each match until Sinjin made me quit." Stephanie popped a piece of nicotine gum in her mouth and began chewing furiously. "When she was a teenager, I could always console her by saying, *There's always next year*, but…"

She didn't finish her sentence. She didn't have to. Laure knew how much was at stake. If Sinjin's knees gave out, there might not be a next year.

❖

The tiebreaker was a reflection of the set—nip and tuck the whole way. The score was tied at six points-all with one more point to go on Sinjin's serve when the players moved to the opposite sides of the court for the traditional change of ends. Sinjin stopped at her chair to towel off. She had just fought off set point. The next point was just as crucial. If she won it, she would have match point. If Rosana took it, she would have set point on her own serve. If Rosana sneaked out the set, the momentum would swing in her direction and she would resume the role of favorite.

"Serve an ace!" someone yelled when Sinjin approached the baseline. The well-intentioned fan was trying to break the tension but ended up adding to it.

Sinjin mustered a smile, then hit her first serve two feet past the service line. The crowd let out a collective groan. Was this the moment Sinjin came back to Earth?

Rosana moved forward, crowding the baseline so she could hit a forceful return.

Sinjin had two choices: go for a big second serve or take something off it to make sure she got the ball in play. Going back and forth with her decision, she didn't make up her mind until she tossed the ball in the air. Out of the corner of her eye, she saw Rosana slide to her left to cut off a serve to her backhand so she decided to serve out wide instead.

Rosana's shoulders slumped after the ball landed safely in the corner of the service box and thumped against the wall at the back of the court. She looked like a marionette whose strings had just been cut.

Match point.

Leaning forward in their seats, Laure and Stephanie clutched each other's hands. They—and the crowd—were ready to explode.

Sinjin slapped her hand against her thigh to remind herself to stay alert. She looked for another tell, but Rosana didn't give anything away.

Rosana's first serve was flat and deep. Too deep. Cyclops, the electronic machine that surveyed an area eighteen inches wide, beeped to indicate the serve was a fault. It was Sinjin's turn to crowd the baseline. Instead of standing just beyond it like most players did when they moved up, she stood just inside it, daring Rosana to hit a deep second serve.

The knowledgeable crowd noted Sinjin's bravery—or foolhardiness.

Unnerved by Sinjin's audacious court positioning, Rosana dumped her second serve into the net.

"Game, set, match, Miss Smythe," the chair umpire said. "Miss Smythe wins two sets to love, six-four, seven-six."

The crowd erupted, but mindful of Rosana's feelings, Sinjin kept her celebration low-key. Winning on a double fault was anticlimactic. Losing on one was devastating.

"Bad luck," Sinjin said when she and Rosana shook hands at the net.

"You were the better player." Rosana gave Sinjin a pat on the back. Even though she wanted to win as badly as anyone else, she was known for being a gracious loser. If a player outperformed her on a given day, she gave the player credit where credit was due. "You deserved it. Good luck the rest of the way."

"Thanks. I appreciate that."

Sinjin impulsively blew a kiss to Laure and Stephanie before raising her arms to acknowledge the cheering crowd.

"Isn't this fun?" she asked as she, Laure, Stephanie, and Kendall walked across the grounds. A cadre of uniformed security guards surrounded them.

"If torture is your idea of fun." Stephanie cast an anxious glance at the large crowd following them.

"I meant the match."

"So did I."

"So I guess we're going to Fog for dinner again?" Stephanie asked.

When she was on a winning streak, Sinjin liked to eat the same meal each night. Last night, she and Stephanie dined at a restaurant a few blocks from Stephanie's apartment. The trendy eatery specialized in modern takes on traditional British comfort food. "Order something you could eat every day," Stephanie had teased her, "because you might be eating it for the next two weeks."

Sinjin's favorite comfort food was fish and chips. Settling for a healthier alternative, she had ordered grilled salmon and twice-baked potatoes.

"How do you know me so well?"

"Lots of practice."

Sinjin paused to sign autographs. Laure followed suit. Fans thrust everything from today's programs to hand-written posters to body parts in their direction.

"Good luck," someone said.

"We love you!" said another.

"Bring it home!"

The crowd surged forward. The uniformed security guards linked arms and tried to hold them back.

Sinjin signed her name so many times her hand began to cramp. Everyone wanted something from her. A souvenir. A handshake. A win. Her countrymen had been disappointed so many times. If she wanted to avoid adding to the long list of hard-fought but valiant defeats, she needed to play for herself, not an entire nation.

"Thank you."

She stepped away from the crowd and waited for Laure, who signed every program and posed for every photograph as if she could keep it up all day. Typical Laure.

Sinjin was slowly beginning to realize Laure wasn't like most players. She wasn't obsessed with what was best for her. She worried about what was best for the tour. She was willing to sign every autograph, shake every sponsor's hand, sit for every interview—provided the questions didn't get too personal. During a match, she competed as hard as anyone. The instant the match ended, though, so did her desire to be better than the person across the net. Then she was the first to lend them a helping hand. Where would she be if Laure hadn't helped her? Not standing in the winner's circle, that's for sure.

"Did Emme win?" she asked, already thinking about her next match.

Kendall consulted her phone, which she was using to keep track of the live scores on the other courts. "She's up a set and two breaks. She's a game away."

"Then I guess I'll see her tomorrow."

Instead of having the day off, the players in the top half of the draw would be right back on court the next day. Sinjin was grateful for the short turnaround. Instead of having too much time to reflect on what she had already accomplished, she could focus on what lay ahead.

"Are you going to stick around for my press conference?"

"I don't think that's a good idea," Laure said. "Yesterday I was asked more questions about you than my match and I'm sure you're going to be given the same treatment today. My presence would make it worse. Give me a call afterward."

"You got it."

❖

Laure rolled a massage bar over her thighs to release the lactic acid in her muscles. She turned on the TV to take her mind off the chore. Sinjin appeared on the screen. Sitting behind a bank of microphones, she faced the assembled press corps.

"Who are you wearing?" a reporter asked.

The question made Laure feel like Sinjin was walking the red carpet instead of sitting in the press room in the Millennium Building, but it afforded Sinjin the opportunity to give Stephanie's fledgling line some free publicity.

"*B and B* by Stephanie Smythe."

The name, Laure knew, was a play on Stephanie's nickname. Stephanie, who had always been accident-prone, spent most of her life covered in bruises. So much so her friends had taken to calling her Black and Blue.

"She has some great looks planned for me," Sinjin said. "I hope I stick around long enough to show them all off."

"Rosana said playing you today was a drag," another journalist began. "Do you think she meant that literally?"

The question was obviously meant to stir up controversy. Laure hoped Sinjin didn't take the bait. She remembered the time she had played Wimbledon through a firestorm. It was the first year she had burst onto the scene and she had upset the top seed in the semifinals by flashing the aggressive game that would soon become her trademark.

"She puts so much pressure on you all the time," the top seed, since retired, had said. "The way she crowds the net and hits winners from all over the court, it's almost like playing a guy out there."

The press had turned the comment on its head, making it seem like the other players considered Laure too masculine to play the women's game. The unwanted attention had shaken her focus. She had played the final as if in a daze. Serena Williams had bulldozed her in just over an hour. But armed with a thicker skin and steadier nerves, she had returned to the site of her collapse the next year and stormed to the title.

"I didn't give Rosana any opportunities to break my serve today," Sinjin said. "So for someone who returns as well as she does, it couldn't have been very much fun for her out there today. That's what I think she meant."

"After failing to qualify for the event, this is a big win for you. How does it feel?"

"Like I'm just getting started."

"Laure Fortescue was in the stands for your matches during qualifying and she was there again today. You were a conspicuous presence in her Friends Box yesterday. Sources say you've been quite close off the court as well. You've been seen leaving her rented house on several occasions. Is there something you wish to share regarding the status of your relationship?"

Laure had known the questions would turn personal. They always did when Sinjin played at home, but she hadn't expected it to happen so quickly.

This is the "reward" she gets for one of the biggest wins of her career?

Sinjin took a sip of water as she paused to formulate an answer to the query. Laure leaned toward the TV. If Sinjin answered the question the wrong way, they'd have reporters and photographers camped out on both their doorsteps for days.

"Laure and I have been friends for years. Nothing has or ever will change that."

Good answer.

"How can you be friends when you both want the same thing? Doesn't a Wimbledon title trump friendship?"

That was one question Sinjin didn't have an answer for.

❖

Sinjin was jubilant. She had faced the firing squad and come out unscathed. Well, relatively. The last question had been a doozy. Some arsehole had tried to equate her knee therapy with blood doping, the illegal performance-enhancing practice that had ruined cycling's reputation worldwide. The other questions hadn't been a walk in the park either. If she had a penny for every time she had used the word *friendship* in her responses, she would be able to buy Windsor Castle. No matter. Her victory over Rosana had put her in the mix. She was a contender now.

She wanted to celebrate. She couldn't remember the last time she had felt so good. Physically or mentally. How long had it been? One year? Two? No matter what the actual number was, way too much time had passed since the last time she felt like she was firing on all cylinders.

She ran into Kendall on her way out of the locker room. Kendall was one of her few remaining single friends. Most of the others were comfortably ensconced in relationships. Kendall would probably never allow herself to be tied down unless there were whips and chains involved.

"Do you want to grab a drink?"

"I'd be happy to help you spend some of the prize money you just won."

Kendall flashed a lopsided grin that should have made Sinjin's stomach turn somersaults. In the past few days, the only smile that had that effect was Laure's. Was the change permanent?

She and Kendall rode the tube to Soho and walked into London's lone women-only bar. A round of applause greeted their arrival. Sinjin had thought her presence would go unnoticed. She basked in the unexpected attention.

"Anything you want is on the house," the bartender said.

"In that case," Kendall said, "we'll have two of everything."

"Down, girl." Sinjin amended Kendall's order. "A bottle of water and a Foster's, please."

"Anything you want," the bartender said. "And I mean anything."

Kendall leaned forward to get a better look at the bartender's butt as she bent to retrieve a can of beer from an ice-filled cooler. Sinjin stayed put.

"You could have told me you and Laure were dating," Kendall said as they nursed their drinks.

"We aren't." Sinjin stared at the TV screen, where Clair Wilkinson—recently touted as the future of British women's tennis—was going down in flames.

Apparently, reports of her rise and my demise were premature.

"Bullshit. Abby told me how you ran out on her because there was 'someplace you had to be.' Then I saw that picture in the *Daily Mail* of you standing on Laure's doorstep with a bottle of wine under your arm. We both know what that means."

"That someone with a telephoto lens didn't have anything better to do that night?" She dragged her eyes away from the one-sided match and looked at Kendall's tanned, perpetually smiling face. "As I said during my press conference, Laure and I have a friendship, not a relationship."

Kendall took a sip of her pale ale. "Nice try, but I refuse to believe that was anything other than a line you trotted out to protect your relationship from further scrutiny. If you want me to believe you, there is a way for you to prove it to me."

"How?" Sinjin raised a bottle of mineral water to her mouth and took a long swallow.

"Come back to my flat with me and help me break in my new bed. My mattress isn't the only thing I have that's rock hard."

Sinjin spit water all over the bar. Kendall grabbed a pile of napkins and helped her sop up the mess.

"Not the reaction I was expecting, but it proves I'm right. You do have something brewing with Laure."

Sinjin looked around to make sure no one in the steadily growing crowd had overheard Kendall's comment. "You can't say anything to anyone. Do you hear me?"

"Mum's the word. I swear." Kendall lowered her voice to a whisper. "Have you done the deed?"

"I haven't even kissed her yet."

"What are you waiting for?"

"Hello?" Sinjin tossed the soaked wads of paper into a trash bin behind the bar. "I have a tournament to win."

"You can't do both? You can't win a tournament and get some action at the same time?"

"I tried that once. It didn't work."

"Because you let Queen Viktoriya walk all over you."

The press had coined Viktoriya's nickname to describe her regal bearing on court. Her fellow players used it to describe her imperious attitude in the locker room.

"You were expected to be her subject, not her equal. She said 'jump' and you said 'how high?' She said—"

"You don't have to remind me," Sinjin said testily. "I was there, remember?" She finished her drink and slammed the empty bottle on the bar. "I've got to go."

"Volley drills in the morning," Kendall said as they stood just outside the front door. "I know they're your favorite, so I'm going to make sure you work your ass off."

"Take it easy on me, okay? I do have a match to play tomorrow afternoon."

"I'll think about it. Now give me a hug and run home to your girlfriend."

Sinjin didn't bother to correct Kendall's slip of the tongue. She gave her a quick kiss and a lingering hug. Then she turned to leave. "Aren't you coming?"

"You might have someone waiting for you at home, but I don't." Kendall turned and walked back into the bar.

Sinjin headed for Stephanie's apartment. As she walked the crowded streets, she thought about the conversation she and Kendall had shared.

Could she do both? Could she win the tournament while she was developing a relationship with one of the players she might have to defeat at some point?

"There's only one way to find out. Let's hope I don't lose both in the process."

❖

Laure's cell phone rang while she and Nicolas were reviewing scouting reports on her next opponent. Gabrielle picked up the phone and read the display.

"It's Sinjin. Shall I send it to voice mail?"

"No." Laure leaped out of her seat. "Give me the phone."

Nicolas cleared his throat. "We aren't finished."

"Anaïs and I have played each other seventeen times. If I don't know her game by now, I never will." She took the phone and jogged upstairs to her bedroom. "Sin?"

"How did I do?"

Sinjin's voice brought an immediate smile to her face. "On the court or in the press room?"

"Either."

"You were aces in both."

"I have something to tell you."

"Uh oh. That sounds ominous."

"Promise you won't get mad."

Laure's heart skipped a beat. Sinjin's press conference had ended hours ago. Where had she been since then, visiting Abby or some other equally willing partner to scratch another itch? Barely any time had passed since they acknowledged their attraction to each other and Sinjin was already beginning to stray?

"Just tell me."

"Kendall figured out what's going on with us."

Laure released her death grip on the edge of the mattress. Sinjin's news wasn't what she wanted to hear, but it was better than what she had feared.

"How did she figure us out when we haven't?"

"Clairvoyant I guess."

"She should add that to her job description. Somewhere between Pilates aficionado and Zumba expert."

"I swore her to secrecy."

"Did she cross her heart and hope to die?" Laure lay back on the bed. She felt like a teenager in the throes of a crush. *Soon I'll start peppering my text messages with emoticons and ending every sentence with LOL or LMAO.*

"You're making light of this? I thought you'd be pissed."

"Unless Kendall's walking around with a tape recorder in her pocket, I don't think we have anything to worry about."

"She's carrying something, but the last time I looked it wasn't a tape recorder."

"When was the last time you looked?" Mireille's cheating had left Laure gun-shy. Sinjin was open about her voracious appetites. Did that make her more suitable as a partner or less?

"It's been a while. To be honest, I haven't looked at anyone since I came to see you last week."

"Is that a personal best?"

"Pretty close."

"I'll buy you a chastity belt for your birthday."

"Only if you promise we can play French Revolution. I'll be Marie Antoinette and you can be Louis XIV."

"You might want to choose a different role. If I remember my history correctly, Marie Antoinette lost her head."

"Then the part's perfect for me. Because I'm definitely losing mine."

"Do you rehearse these lines or do they come naturally to you?"

"I'll admit that wasn't my best effort. Let me go back to the drawing board and see what I can do."

"You do that."

Laure was glad they weren't talking via Skype. If they were, Sinjin would have seen her blush. No one else got to her this way. No one else put her at ease while at the same time keeping her on her toes.

"Are you going to the dog and pony show tomorrow night?" Sinjin asked.

They were sponsored by the same racquet company. With most of the tennis world gathered in London, representatives of the firm had planned a lavish gala at the London Eye, the popular tourist attraction that dominated the waterfront's skyline.

Laure traced a finger over a rose embroidered in the floral-themed duvet. "The last time I looked, our presence was required, not expected."

"Would you like to go together?"

"Are you asking me on a date?"

"If you want to call it that."

"Sure. If I'm going to be trapped in a slow-moving capsule for an hour, I'd rather it be with someone whose company I actually enjoy."

"Not the most enthusiastic 'yes' I've ever received, but I'll take it."

They talked for a while longer before ending the call. Laure floated downstairs. Nicolas took note of her ear-to-ear grin.

"I'm glad you're happy, but I don't want you to lose focus."

Laure tossed the scouting reports on the coffee table and reached for her sketchpad. "My match isn't until Thursday. *If* I've lost focus, I've got time to find it."

SECOND ROUND

Sinjin's knees were fine, but her back was killing her. Stephanie's oversized couch was more comfortable than some hotel beds she had slept in, but it wasn't the Four Seasons. Or the Ritz-Carlton. Then again, she hadn't done much sleeping that night.

Last night she had fallen asleep watching video of her match against Emme during the qualifying tournament. Now she had the heavily hyped rematch to play and her muscles were tied up in knots. So was her stomach.

Emme had drubbed a fellow qualifier in the first round to set up the match all of England wanted to see. The winner would most likely play Anke Schroeder, who had upset the twenty-fifth seed in the first round and was favored to defeat the previous year's junior champion in the second.

Stephanie put the empty breakfast plates in the dishwasher and strode to the corded phone nestled in a cubby hole next to the front door. The phone was connected to the buzzer downstairs. A small screen above the phone displayed images from the security camera above the building's front door.

Stephanie picked up the phone, listened for a second or two and said, "She'll be right down." After hanging up, she reached for her suit jacket and shrugged it on. "Your courtesy car's here."

The All England Lawn Tennis Club provided a fleet of compact SUVs to shuttle the players between the tournament site and the players' temporary accommodations, alleviating them of at least one headache. They couldn't do anything about the matches themselves—or the often iffy weather.

Sinjin quickly downed the rest of her coffee and joined Stephanie by the front door. "I'll see you later, yeah?"

"I have meetings all morning, but I'll be in the stands by the time your match starts. Tell Nicolas to save me a seat. Good luck this afternoon." Stephanie wrapped her arms around Sinjin's neck. "God, you're tense. I feel like I'm hugging a statue." She briskly rubbed Sinjin's arms and shoulders. "If you're worried about today, don't be. You don't have to prove you belong. You already did that yesterday. Just go out there and kick Emme's arse."

"I'll try."

Stephanie tilted her head. "Are you okay?"

Sinjin rubbed her aching back. "I think I'm getting too old for your couch."

"Try using the bed next time. That's what it's for."

"Thanks, sis. I'll try to remember that."

She followed Stephanie downstairs and climbed into the back of the courtesy car. The driver whisked her across town and parked in front of the players' entrance. Sinjin showed her ID badge to one of the guards at the security checkpoint, then placed her racquet bag and duffel bag on a table so they could be searched.

Her match was the third one scheduled for Court Eight, which meant she probably wouldn't begin play until after four o'clock. The forgiving schedule would give her plenty of time to have a training session with Kendall, a light practice session with her hitting partner, a rubdown from the tour masseuse, and a leisurely lunch in the players' lounge.

After changing clothes in the locker room, she headed to the practice courts at Aorangi Park. Kendall was waiting for her.

Kendall picked up a medicine ball. "Chuck this around and get those muscles loose."

They tossed the six-pound ball back and forth. Sinjin caught it first on her left side then her right, swinging her body from side to side to warm up her core. As she gradually worked up a sweat, she thought about her upcoming match.

The last time she played Emme, she had converted only two of ten break point opportunities. If she played the big points that poorly again, Emme would bounce her out of the tournament just like she had in Roehampton. Only this time there would be no second chances.

"Last one," Kendall said. "Make it good."

The force of Sinjin's throw drove Kendall backward.

"Easy, tiger. Don't sprain all ten of my fingers. I may need my hands later."

Andrew ambled over. His weathered face and skinny, bowed legs made him look more like a leprechaun than a tennis coach. He ran a hand through his thinning silver hair. "All right. Let's get to work."

Sinjin honed her game under his watchful eye.

Though long retired, Andrew had agreed to help her attempt to refine the raw talent he had first spotted so long ago. She had called him the day after the final round of qualifying matches at Roehampton. He had immediately volunteered his services—with one caveat. He would oversee her practice sessions as long as he didn't have to sit courtside during her matches.

Sinjin had readily agreed to the unusual—and probably temporary—arrangement. Andrew had been a father figure for her during her formative years after her biological one hit the bricks. She was just happy to have him in her life again even if, at the moment, he was making her life hell.

"You're cheating on those low volleys. When I say, 'bend,' I mean with your legs, not your back." He demonstrated the proper technique, practically scraping his knee on the court as he brought his leg parallel to the ground. "If you get grass stains on those fancy new clothes of yours, it won't be the end of the world. Everything comes out in the wash."

Though his words sounded harsh, his voice was as warm as ever. That didn't stop them from bursting Sinjin's balloon, however. She thought she had played a perfect match when she upset Rosana. According to Andrew, she still had room for improvement. Lots of room.

She had forgotten it took alligator skin to work with him. She had to be careful not to let his blunt critiques dent her confidence. Sometimes one word was all it took to shake her self-belief. She could feel like a world-beater one second and a rank amateur the next. The flaw had kept her from building on her sensational rookie year. It had helped grease the skids as she slid down the rankings. Her injuries had provided built-in excuses. The real reason for the downturn in her career wasn't her body but her head. Viktoriya was inside it and she couldn't get her out.

No one was better at shaking her confidence than Viktoriya Vasilyeva. Viktoriya was an expert at planting seeds of doubt. She was the queen of backhanded compliments. If Sinjin could beat her once—just once—she could turn the tide in their rivalry. She could close the book on years of frustration and begin writing a new chapter.

"Rosana let you get away with a couple of loose volleys yesterday because it was the first round and she was so nervous she couldn't breathe," Andrew said. "Don't expect Emme to let you off the hook today. She beat you once and, in her mind, she thinks she can do it again."

Sinjin set her jaw. "She's wrong."

Andrew allowed himself a rare smile. "That's the spirit."

Laure hung out in the players' lounge while she waited for her scheduled practice court to open up. Sinjin had just finished her practice session and was enjoying a pre-match snack. A grilled chicken sandwich, a bowl of pasta salad, an apple, a couple bananas, and a large bottle of water crowded the tray in her hands. All were better options than the fare offered to fans in the food court, where—aside from the ever-popular strawberries and cream—only the worst of British cuisine crowded the menu.

While they waited, Laure and her trainer Gabrielle Meunier pored through some of the latest tabloids. Sinjin avoided the tabs like the plague, but Laure couldn't resist their cleverly worded headlines. Filled with puns and double entendres, they were always good for a laugh—except when the joke was at her expense.

"The reviews of Chandler's movie are in," Gabrielle said, her nose buried in *The Times*. "To quote one, 'Unintentional comedy is not pretty.'"

Laure was happy to see the reviews for Stephanie's clothing line were much more positive. Stephanie was like the big sister she had never had. Laure adored her. What was not to like? Stephanie was stylish, sophisticated, and funny as hell. But she wasn't Sinjin. Sexy, charming, maddening Sinjin.

Sinjin was a study in contrasts. Underneath the jokes and one-liners lay a soft center she let only a few people see. She could blow off adults who asked for her autograph but never turned down a child who made the same request. Her swagger on court projected a self-confidence she didn't always feel. She shared her body but refused to do the same with her heart. Laure wanted to be the one who helped her meld the disparate halves of her personality into one. She wanted to be the one Sinjin finally gave her heart to, freely and without remorse. To receive it, she had to be able to do the same.

"Let me see that one." She reached for a sports daily Gabrielle had cast aside. *The Kiss-Off*, the headline read. There were two photos beneath the headline. One was of Sinjin blowing a kiss to her supporters in the stands. In the other, Sinjin and Kendall were kissing on a busy sidewalk. "You two make a cute couple."

Laure turned the newspaper around so Sinjin and Kendall could see the front page. Kendall nearly choked on the big bite of apple in her mouth. "Crikey, that's not how it looks. That's not how it was. We were just—"

"Ramming your tongues down each other's throats from the looks of it."

❖

The voice came from behind her.

Sinjin turned to face Viktoriya Vasilyeva. Viktoriya had dropped only one game in the opening round—a dominating performance matched only by Blake Freeman, who had humiliated her first round opponent by double bageling her on Centre Court.

Viktoriya wasn't scheduled to play her next match until the following day. She had come to the club for a training session and was on her way out. Sinjin had spotted her on an adjacent court earlier but had not acknowledged her presence. Now she couldn't be ignored.

"I saw you on the practice court. You looked good out there." Viktoriya tossed her long blond hair over her shoulder, a move that always turned the teenage boys in the stands into puddles of hormone-rich goo during her matches. The way her nipples poked at the material of her tight, sweat-darkened T-shirt used to do the same thing to Sinjin. "Then again, you always look good in practice. Too bad you aren't able to play well when it counts."

"Tori."

Viktoriya's eyebrows shot up as if she were surprised to hear Sinjin use the term of endearment.

Sinjin said something in Russian.

Viktoriya's brow furrowed as her face clouded with fury. Muttering something about "Ungrateful wastes of talent," she whirled around and stomped toward the locker room, her coach, agent, and hitting partner trailing in her wake.

Laure set the newspaper aside. "What did you say to her?"

"'Leave now or I'll put my fist through your fucking face.' Or something to that effect. I can't guarantee nothing was lost in translation."

Kendall laughed so loud people at the surrounding tables craned their necks to see what she had found so amusing. "Good one, mate. I have someplace I have to be—wink, wink—so I'll see you later."

Gabrielle pushed her chair away from the table. "And I need to check on your practice court, Laure, before Nicolas has someone's head."

Sinjin and Laure found themselves alone. Or as close to it as possible in a room filled with hundreds of people.

"She still gets to you, doesn't she?" Laure asked.

Sinjin smiled wanly. "More than you know."

"Do you want to talk about it?"

"Maybe when we're old and gray. Not right now. I can't afford the distraction."

Laure drummed her fingers on the tabletop, her chin resting on the heel of her hand. "What am I? Am I a distraction as well?"

"No." Sinjin rested her hand on Laure's, stilling her restless fingers. "You're better than I deserve."

Laure's dour expression didn't change, but her eyes blazed. Sinjin saw hope blossom in their depths. Despite that encouraging sign, she felt unsettled when she took the court later that afternoon.

As the fans continued to file into their seats, she took a deep breath and tried to calm down. The time would come to let her emotions take over, but this wasn't it. She channeled them into her game instead. Her anger, her stress, her fear. All her feelings flowed through her when she played, transferring from her hand to her racquet to the ball. The court was her safe haven. Her sanctuary. Nothing could touch her as long as she was standing between the painted lines.

When play began, she felt safe. Protected. Invincible. She trounced Emme 6-2, 6-1 in under an hour.

"Perhaps we should have Viktoriya piss you off every day," Laure said afterward.

"No," Sinjin said, wondering how much the day's emotional upheaval would affect her in the next round. "Let's not."

"Are we still on for tonight? I could think of an excuse if you'd like to skip the party."

"No," Sinjin said firmly. "The time for excuses is over. I'll see you tonight."

❖

Laure joined Sinjin at the edge of the crowded capsule. The glass pod held up to twenty-five people and it was filled to capacity. "Regular or unleaded?"

"I have tomorrow off. You don't." Sinjin reached for the glass of champagne, leaving Laure with the mineral water. She pointed at the panorama outside the clear glass walls. "Amazing, isn't it?"

The view from the 443-foot London Eye was spectacular enough to render one speechless. Each of the thirty-two transparent capsules offered unobstructed 360-degree views of the city. On a clear day, passengers could see up to twenty-five miles in all directions as The Eye moved at a snail-like .6 miles per hour. Formerly known as the Millennium Wheel, the architectural wonder rotated continuously, affording riders one of a kind aerial views of, among others, Buckingham Palace, the Houses of Parliament, Battersea Power Station, and the countryside beyond. At the moment, Laure and Sinjin were being treated to the awe-inspiring sight of a picture-perfect sunset as the sun sank over the Thames. When they weren't posing for pictures with dignitaries who wanted face time with a celebrity.

Sinjin looked at the gathered executives. "How much longer do we have to play nice?"

Laure discreetly consulted the sleek designer watch on her wrist. Barely fifteen minutes had passed since the doors had closed and The Eye had been set in slow motion. "You don't want to know." She touched her glass to Sinjin's. "Welcome to the third round."

"I would say the same, but you have some work to do."

In her next match, Laure would square off against Anaïs Chouinard, a former Wimbledon finalist whose game—and ranking—had seen better days. "I'm not going to break our date. Are you?"

"I wasn't planning on it."

Sinjin sounded confident, but she looked as if she were in over her head. Laure knew the feeling. She was in uncharted territory, too. She was falling for another player. And she was falling hard.

"How is it you wine experts are able to tell what's what about a vintage simply by tasting it?" Sinjin asked.

"Patience, practice, and a strong liver."

"No, really. I want to know."

Laure was pleasantly surprised by Sinjin's desire to become informed on a subject about which she was so passionate. Sinjin usually dismissed her other passions—antiques, history, and art—as boring.

"There are five things to look for. The first is color."

She closed her fingers around Sinjin's. Sinjin's warm skin provided a sharp contrast to the chilled glass. Laure's own skin prickled from the heat.

She raised the champagne flute and tipped it toward Sinjin.

"Tilting the glass at an angle lets you see the colors, which can give you clues to the variety of grape the vintner used." She raised the glass to eye level and examined the bubbling champagne. "This test works best on a medium- or full-bodied red like a Syrah or a cabernet instead of champagne, but we'll make do."

She loosened her grip on Sinjin's fingers but didn't release them. She was enjoying the contact too much to sever the connection. She raised the glass higher.

"The second stage is swirl. Swirling the wine exposes it to more oxygen and releases the aromatic molecules that make up its bouquet. We'll skip this step because champagne is a sparkling wine. Swirling would release more bubbles and ruin the bouquet."

"Aromatic molecules, huh? If all my teachers looked like you, Professor Fortescue, I would have paid more attention in school."

Laure moved her hand to Sinjin's wrist. She stroked the sensitive area on the underside. She could feel Sinjin's pulse racing. Or was that hers?

A camera flashed nearby, but she didn't pull away. The dangerous game of cat and mouse she and Sinjin were playing was completely out of character for her—and utterly liberating.

"A wine's nose determines the drinker's perception of its flavor. Once you taste it—once you take it into your mouth—the aromatics are exposed to body heat and burst against your tongue."

Sinjin's breath caught. Her eyes widened ever so slightly. "Are we still talking about wine?"

Laure raised the glass to Sinjin's lips. "Take a sip. Taste the flavors. Let the champagne flow over your tongue. Let it saturate your taste buds. Feel the weight of it. Feel its length."

Sinjin nearly choked on her drink. "Damn," she said, wiping her chin, "I think I just came."

Laure dipped a finger into Sinjin's glass. Sinjin watched her intently as she raised the finger to her lips and slowly licked the tip. "How was the finish?"

"I'm craving a cigarette and I don't even smoke. Does that tell you anything?"

"Then I won't ask you about the afterglow. I mean aftertaste." Laure let the champagne infuse her senses. "I'm getting notes of citrus, vanilla, honey, and toast." She paused. "Pommery Brut Royal. Ten years old. No, eleven."

Sinjin looked astonished. "You barely tasted it. How the hell did you know that?"

Laure grinned. "I read the label while the bartender poured your glass."

"Unfair. Patently unfair." Sinjin took another sip of her champagne. "I had no idea wine tasting could be so sexy. Or maybe it's just you."

Laure rolled her eyes. "Are all your lines this bad?"

"No, I have some that are even worse."

"I can't wait to hear them."

"If I said you had a beautiful body, would you hold it against me? Or how about this one? You must be tired because you've been running through my mind all night."

As she listened to Sinjin recite one wretched pick-up line after another, Laure sipped her Perrier and gave her the once-over. Not for the first time. No matter how hard she tried, she couldn't keep her eyes off her. Sinjin's long hair was swept up and pinned into a loose bun. Two dreads, which had been allowed to remain free, framed her face. And what a face it was. Her makeup was subtle but stunning. Her lips were painted an enticing shade of plum. Blush a few shades darker than her cinnamon-colored skin made her high cheekbones look even higher. Black tuxedo pants showed off her long legs. A sequined black halter-style blouse drew attention to her strong arms.

"You look incredible tonight. More of Stephanie's line?"

"I said she had some great looks planned for me."

"When her designs make it to the stores, they won't be on the shelves for long."

"I'll tell her you said so. I love you in that dress. Though I can't figure out which view I like best. The front or the back." She took Laure's hand and spun her in a circle as if they were partners in a ballroom dancing contest.

Laure was wearing a basic black dress that didn't look so basic when she turned around and revealed the deeply plunging back. Gabrielle had picked it out. The dress wasn't really Laure's style—she would have preferred jeans and a T-shirt—but she liked the dress a little more each time someone said, "Picture, please," and Sinjin's hand brushed across her bare skin before settling into the small of her back.

Sinjin rubbed her neck as if it ached. Earlier that day, she had mentioned feeling stiff and sore after falling asleep on Stephanie's couch. Had her post-match rubdown not been enough to work out the kinks?

"Here. Let me." She placed their empty glasses on a passing waiter's tray. Then she reached up and massaged the back of Sinjin's neck, feeling the tension melt away beneath her fingers. Sinjin's tight body thrummed with energy. Like a bullet waiting to be fired or a thoroughbred yearning to run free. Sinjin groaned when Laure's thumbs dug into the bunched muscles in her shoulders. Then Laure felt Sinjin's energy change. She felt it find focus.

Sinjin turned around. "If you don't stop that, I'm going to make a public spectacle out of you. Although you would enjoy it immensely at the time, you might kill me later."

Laure played innocent. "What could you possibly do to me while we're suspended one hundred thirty-five meters in the air?"

Sinjin reached for her. For a moment, Laure thought she meant to pull her into her arms. To grab a handful of her hair and hold her in place. To lean down and press her mouth to hers. Instead, she turned her around and pretended to repair a broken clasp on the strand of pearls around her neck.

"First, I'd do this."

She ran her fingers through the downy-soft hairs on the nape of Laure's neck. The sensation was electric. Laure pressed her lips together to keep from crying out.

"Then I'd do this." She slid one hand from the nape of Laure's neck to the base of her spine.

Laure felt her control begin to slip.

"Then I'd replace my fingers with my tongue."

Laure tried to turn around, but Sinjin held her in place. She brought her mouth close to Laure's ear.

"I want to feel your body arch underneath mine. I want to move with you. Against you. I want to hear you scream my name again and again, then beg for more. We could do that here or we could go back to your place. What do you say?"

Laure rubbed the back of her neck to make the tingling stop. She could still feel Sinjin's breath blowing whisper-soft against her skin. "I say we need to revisit this conversation at a later date."

"After you're retired and we're no longer in direct competition? That's six months from now."

"Good things come to those who wait."

Laure fired a ball against the back of the court. She had twice as many errors as winners in a match that wasn't as close as the score indicated. She had just lost her serve to go down a break in the second set. She had already lost the first set 6-4. If Anaïs had taken advantage of even half the opportunities she had given her, the match would already be over.

The crowd, sensing an upset, began to buzz. Was Laure about to become the highest women's seed to fall?

She stared at the scoreboard as she waited for the chair umpire to call time. She was down a set and 3-2. If she didn't get her act together soon, her dream of a second Wimbledon title would come to a premature end.

She jogged to the baseline as Anaïs prepared to serve to extend her lead. The crowd roared when Laure won the first point. She clenched her fist and glanced at her supporters in the Friends Box. "Let's go," Nicolas and Gabrielle yelled in unison. Next to them sat her parents, Henri and Mathilde. Unlike most tennis parents, who were omnipresent during tournaments, her mother and father normally attended championship matches only. Aware this was her last time playing Wimbledon, they had come to England early, arriving via Chunnel that afternoon.

Drawing energy from the crowd and strength from her parents' presence, Laure tried to claw her way back into the match. She wasted two break points, though, and Anaïs held serve. Anaïs was two games from the match. And Laure was two games from going home.

❖

Sinjin stepped on the balcony outside Centre Court. The area was called the Crow's Nest, but the only birds who flocked there were vultures—agents trying to make deals and players watching their rivals struggle on the courts that sat a few feet below.

She elbowed her way between a player scouting his next opponent and an agent working his cell phone to claim a place near the railing. She would have to support Laure from a distance. Court Five was packed. Not a seat to be had. She looked at the hand-operated scoreboard. Anaïs was up 6-4, 5-4. When the changeover ended, she would serve for the match.

"Come on. You can do this."

She didn't know she had said the words out loud until Viktoriya sidled up to her side and said, "Are you rooting for Laure to win or lose? Neither she nor Anaïs are in your side of the draw and neither one has a chance in hell of beating me, so what does it matter to you, anyway? Besides, if Laure lost, she'd do us both a favor. She'd be out of my hair as well as yours. You wouldn't have to wring your hands over the prospect of playing her in a final neither of you is going to reach. So be honest. Aren't you rooting for Anaïs just a little bit?"

Sinjin hated to admit it, but there was an element of truth in what Viktoriya was saying. If Laure lost, she wouldn't have to worry about competing against her if they reached the championship match. With Laure out of the tournament, she would have one less player to worry about. But she didn't want to see Laure hurt. A loss this early would devastate her whether it was her last Wimbledon or her first.

Sinjin faced Viktoriya for the second time in as many days. "What I said yesterday still stands."

Viktoriya smirked, her ice blue eyes dancing with merriment. She didn't look like a woman in danger of losing her number one ranking. She looked like her old self. "I'm not afraid of you, Sinjin. You may talk a big game, but I know you're a pussycat underneath it all." She leaned forward until her lips were inches from Sinjin's ear. "I saw the way you looked at me in the players' lounge yesterday," she said in Russian. "You still want me. Let me make you purr, pussy."

Sinjin gripped the railing as if the safety structure were a life preserver preventing her from going under. Viktoriya's offer should have been easy to refuse. Why wasn't she saying no? When Viktoriya trailed a finger across the back of her hand, she felt her body begin to betray her. Quick, no-strings sex was her favorite outlet for relieving tension. Heaven knew she was about to blow. But for the first time in a long time, what she wanted wasn't what she needed. She needed—and wanted—Laure.

"I've learned some things since we were together," Viktoriya said. "I would love to show them to you."

"I would love to show you something, too. My back as I walk away. I hope you enjoy the view."

Sinjin hoped to get in the last word. Viktoriya, as usual, one-upped her.

"I always do. There's nothing like the view from the top."

❖

As she sat in her chair during the changeover, Laure took a sip of water and looked around. The court was standing room only. So was the Crow's Nest. The vultures were circling. Let them circle. She wasn't dead yet.

She took another sip of water. And nearly choked on it when she spotted Sinjin and Viktoriya conversing. Though calling it conversing was a stretch. Viktoriya seemed to be doing most of the talking. Sinjin's body language screamed "Go away," but Viktoriya kept moving closer.

Sinjin walked away, but Viktoriya's broad smile said she had gotten what she wanted. Or soon would. Turning that smile in Laure's direction, she held up her hand and waved. Was she waving hello or good-bye?

"You can't get rid of me that easily, your highness. You and I have a date in the semifinals."

She broke Anaïs' serve at love, then went on a tear. She couldn't miss. No shot was impossible. She won the second set 7-5 and closed out the match in dominant fashion, finishing with her sixth ace as she won the third set 6-0.

"The match was closer than most people anticipated," a reporter said during the press conference that followed. "What happened?"

"Anaïs played well from the beginning of the match and I didn't play as well as I'm capable of until the match was almost over. She hit some good shots and kept me off balance for almost two sets. I was a bit lucky to pull out the second set. I've been working on beefing up my serve. In the third set, it finally began to pay dividends. The match wasn't pretty, but a win's a win and I'll take it."

"I noticed Sinjin Smythe wasn't in attendance today. Will you explain why?"

"Just because you didn't see her didn't mean she wasn't around. She has a match to prepare for. She can't do that by sitting around watching me struggle for two and a half hours."

"Will you be in the stands for her match tomorrow?"

"Of course. This is my—" She barely stopped herself from saying *last*. "This is one of my favorite tournaments and I want to spend it surrounded by the people I care about. Sinjin's one of those people."

❖

Sitting on the couch in Laure's rented house, Sinjin cued up a replay of the 1986 U.S. Open semifinal between Martina Navratilova and Steffi Graf. Navratilova had won the classic match 10-8 in the third set tiebreaker against the upstart Graf who would go on to claim twenty-two Grand Slam singles titles, second only to Australian great Margaret Smith Court's twenty-four.

Laure looked over Sinjin's shoulder. "Why are you watching a hard court match to prepare for one on grass? The styles of play dictated by the two surfaces are completely different."

In the next round, Sinjin would be squaring off against Anke Schroeder. The winner would advance to the round of sixteen for the first time in her career.

"To remind myself of something."

"What?"

"That."

She pointed to the computer monitor. Laure peered at the action on the screen.

Preparing to deliver a second serve at eight points-all in the third set tiebreaker after failing to convert three match points, seventeen-year-old Graf was so nervous she couldn't hold on to her racquet as she stood at the baseline.

"I have to keep telling myself Anke will hit her share of winners tomorrow, but at some point, she will eventually remember she's only eighteen. I just have to hang in there long enough to be in position to take advantage of the moment when it arrives."

She closed the file and opened one that contained footage of the same players' clash in the following year's Wimbledon final. The match was less complicated than its predecessor, but it had meant much more. History—and the number one ranking—had been on the line. In the end, Steffi had eventually taken Martina's top spot, but on that day, Martina's kick serves to Steffi's backhand had carried her to her sixth consecutive Wimbledon title and eighth overall. She would earn a record ninth three years later. Sinjin turned the sound down, letting the images flow across the screen *sans* commentary.

"How was your day?" she asked.

"Frustrating, but I managed to get through it. That's what counts. On the brighter side, Nicolas told me he asked Stephanie to dinner."

Sinjin was only mildly surprised. She had seen the way Nicolas looked at Stephanie over the years—and Stephanie at him. The interest was definitely mutual. The only question was how far Stephanie would allow the relationship to develop before she reverted to her usual MO and found an excuse to end it.

"You'll never guess what I got in the mail today," Sinjin said.

"An offer to change your mobile phone provider?"

Sinjin pulled an envelope out of her laptop bag and tossed it to Laure. "No, try again."

Laure turned the envelope over in her hands but didn't reach for what was inside. "What's this?"

"A letter from the Queen."

"Oh? Did you forget to pay your taxes?"

"No, she said if I make the final, she'll come to watch me play."

Laure's eyes widened. The only sporting events the Queen regularly attended were The Derby and the Royal Ascot. She never missed England's most prestigious horse race, but aside from the Duke of Kent and the late Princess Diana, the sight of a Windsor at the All England Club was as rare as a Wimbledon without rain. "I thought she hated tennis."

"She does."

"So I guess it's up to you to change her mind." Laure nudged Sinjin's hip with her foot. "Good luck with that."

"Thanks. I appreciate the support."

"I'm here for you. Do you really think she'll come?"

"She said she would. Why would she lie?"

"She is a politician after all."

"Then I guess there's only one way to find out for sure: make the final and see if she shows up." She leaned back on the couch and sighed.

Laure hugged her knees to her chest. "Would you rather be off painting the town red instead of listening to Stephanie, Gabrielle, and my parents discuss the merits of paisley versus plaid while Nicolas tries not to burn the steaks? Excuse me. Six steaks and one lonely salmon filet."

"I've already risked jinxing myself by having dinner here instead of at Fog. You managed to get me here, but there's no way you're going to convince me to change my meal, too."

"Relax. I'm not trying to play mind games with you. I just wanted to spend some time with you without talking about anything remotely related to tennis."

Taking the hint, Sinjin shut down her laptop.

"This nuclear family thing is new to me. I haven't been part of a traditional family since I was little. My father left when I was four. My mother died when I was thirteen. My father's parents took care of Steph and me for a while. I've lived in the States off and on since I enrolled at a tennis academy in Florida when I was fifteen. Stephanie moved out on her own shortly after. For years, it's been the two of us against the world, and we didn't see each other as much as we should because I was traveling all the time. Both of us have been alone more often than not."

"Has your father ever tried to reach out to you? My parents and I are so close I can't imagine not having either of them around."

"I haven't seen my dad since I was sixteen. He showed up at one of my junior tournaments and stuck around long enough to say hi then took off again. When Steph and I were kids, he would call us on our birthdays and say he was coming to see us, but he never showed up. After a while, we stopped caring. We had a mother who loved us, we had each other, and we didn't need anyone else."

"But your grandparents are still in your life. I remember you telling me how your father's parents tape your matches and watch them after they've ended."

"Even though they already know the result by the time they watch the tapes, my grandfather still yells at the screen as if he can affect the outcome and my grandmother makes enough pots of tea to supply an army." She laughed at the fond memory. "My mother's parents are just as bad. I've offered to get all of them tickets for some of my matches, but they're just like Andrew—so nervous they can't watch in person. My paternal grandparents are in Brighton, but my maternal ones are still in Nigeria. I don't see my mother's parents as often as I do my father's, obviously, but I do keep in touch with them. The last time I talked to them, they said all of Lagos was cheering for me."

"Great," Laure said with a wink. "Like you weren't enough of a crowd favorite already."

Sinjin shrugged as she basked in the glow of Laure's smile. "Everyone loves an underdog."

"I'm rather fond of them, too."

"I think I can do this."

"What? Win the tournament?"

"No." She leaned forward and kissed Laure's cheek. "Fall in love with you."

THIRD ROUND

L aure thought the best part of a relationship was having someone to share things with. From something as simple as a meal to something as profound as a work of art. She wanted someone to share her life with the way her parents had been sharing theirs for the past forty years. Her mother was a curator for the Louvre. Her father was an art dealer who specialized in emerging artists. She had grown up listening to their lively debates about food, wine, music, and art. Their latest talking point was Picasso's *Child With a Dove*. She smiled to herself as she watched them debate the merits of the portrait while speculating about the "secret" painting that might be hidden under the thick layers of oil. As she stood in line to see Van Gogh's *Sunflowers*, she wished she could emulate their example. She wished Sinjin was by her side.

Her parents provided pleasant company as they spent the day exploring the endless treasures housed in the National Gallery, but she couldn't stop wondering what Sinjin would make of them all.

What would she have to say about Rubens' *Samson and Delilah*? Would Sinjin, as she had, find areas of confluence in Cézanne's *Bathers* and Seurat's similarly-titled *Bathers at Asnières*? Would she prefer them to Monet's *Bathers at La Grenouillère*? Would she be entranced by Velázquez' *Rokeby Venus* or would she be drawn instead to Ingres' haughty *Madame Moitessier*? Would she aspire to have her likeness hang alongside those of other notable Britons in the National Portrait Gallery? Or would she be bored to tears by the whole thing?

Someone in line behind her gently tapped her on the shoulder. "You're Laure Fortescue, aren't you?"

Laure turned to face her inquisitor, a cute redhead in a pinstriped suit, stiletto heels, and a lacy blouse that invited further inspection. Then she took a quick glance around to see how many people might swoop down on her if she said yes. She liked spending time with her fans, but she'd rather spend this day with her family. Just like Sinjin, she didn't see her family nearly as often as she wanted. Another reason to look forward to retirement. When her playing days were over, she and her parents could try to regain some of the time they had lost. She couldn't wait for them to be together for days or even weeks at a time, either at their apartment in Paris or her house in Saint Tropez.

"Yes, I am."

"I thought it was you. Thrilling win yesterday."

Laure reflexively gripped the sketchbook in her hands. The only thing she wanted to take away from the previous round was the fact that she had won. Everything else was best forgotten. "A little too thrilling, if you ask me."

"You'll play better when you're back on the show courts. I imagine it must be difficult to concentrate with the excitement and hubbub of seven other courts in action all around you. Speaking of excited, Sinjin has a lot of people's pulses racing."

Mine included.

"Do you think she can go all the way?"

"She has a tough draw," Laure said, "but if she plays up to her abilities, she can do some damage."

"That would be lovely to see. Tell her we're all rooting for her. All of us."

"I will."

She inched closer to Van Gogh's Impressionist masterpiece. In another week, she hoped to paint a masterpiece of her own. And it could come at Sinjin's expense.

A roar swept across the room.

"Unless a long-lost Gainsborough has been found," Laure said to no one in particular, "I fear we've missed something."

The redhead consulted her smartphone. "Ah, Andy Murray just advanced to the round of sixteen."

"Good for him."

Murray was poised to make another deep run. Would he stall in the semifinals yet again or was he finally ready to break through to his first Wimbledon final?

After she made her way through the line and got a good, long look at the painting, she headed to the espresso bar downstairs. Her parents joined her a few minutes later. While her mother viewed digital reproductions of the gallery's collection via a state-of-the-art touch screen, her father reached for her sketchbook. "Let's see what you've been working on this week."

"It's not finished yet." She tried to grab the book, but he pulled it out of her reach.

He arched an eyebrow. "Are you doubting my ability to judge a work in progress?"

"Of course not, but I'd rather show you the finished product." She took another swipe at the sketchbook, but he leaned away from her.

"Indulge him," her mother said with a well-practiced sigh.

Laure tore her paper napkin into shreds as her father slowly flipped through the pages. He rubbed his chin as he examined the last page in the sketchbook. She recognized the look. It was the same look that crossed his face every time he examined a work that intrigued him.

"Hmph." The familiar grunt was a mixture of appreciation and pride.

Her mother leaned over to take a peek. "Extraordinary. Do you have a title?"

"Medusa."

"Fitting," her father said, sliding the sketchbook across the table. "I look forward to seeing the completed work. And to continuing to get to know your subject."

After the final point of each of her matches, Sinjin removed the bandanna that held her hair out of her eyes. When she shook her hair free, she always reminded Laure of the gorgon from Greek mythology. Only Laure didn't turn to stone when she looked into her eyes. She turned to mush instead. Her sketch depicted Sinjin in all her hair-flying glory. She traced a finger across the nearly finished drawing, being careful not to smudge the hatch lines.

Warm fingers grazed the nape of her neck, sending chills down her spine. She turned, half-hoping Sinjin had decided to brave a potential mob scene in order to surprise her. The cute redhead with the stiletto heels held a business card between two French-tipped fingers.

"In case you need additional tennis results."

Laure glanced at the card, which identified its owner as Sienna Armstrong, corporate accounts representative for one of London's largest banks.

"Good luck tomorrow," Sienna said.

"Thank you."

"My pleasure."

"Hmph," Laure's father grunted after Sienna took her leave. "The Fortescue charm strikes again. She gets it from me, you know."

"Thankfully," Laure's mother said as Laure passed her the card under the table, "she gets her discretion from me." She palmed the card and deposited it in the nearest trash bin.

Laure knew she would be fantasizing about those stiletto heels for days. In her dreams, the woman wearing them wouldn't be Sienna Armstrong but Sinjin Smythe.

Sinjin toed the baseline. Anke was too talented a returner to give her free games and hope to be able to catch up. Holding serve was imperative. Sinjin hadn't had her serve broken in her first two matches. She hadn't even faced break point. Now in the very first game, she found herself staring at three of them.

She erased the break points with back-to-back-to-back aces, then struck a service winner to reach game point. Before she could put the anxious crowd's fears to rest, though, Anke drew the game to deuce with a return that whizzed past her before she was barely out of her service motion.

Okay, she thought as she looked around Court Two, *it's going to be a long day at the office.*

Sensing she needed an energy boost, the crowd broke into rhythmic applause.

Sinjin bounced on her toes, reminding herself to move her feet. She tried to pump herself up, but she felt flat. By making the third round, she had achieved a personal best. She had reached one of the goals she had set for herself before the tournament began. But that modest goal was no longer enough. She wanted more. And she would have to do it at the expense of a friend.

She looked across the net at Anke. So young, so eager. Her hunger to win was fully evident. For the first time in the tournament, Sinjin didn't feel that hunger in herself. What she felt was the fear of losing. She didn't want to walk off the court second best, but at the same time, she didn't want to be responsible for dashing Anke's dreams.

When she double faulted to give Anke another break point, she felt as if she was reverting to her old self.

"Dig deep." Laure pounded her fist over her heart. "Whatever it takes. Win this and you get two days off."

Sinjin had tried to conserve energy in the first two rounds to save herself for the later ones. But with no play scheduled for Sunday, the traditional day of rest, she was in a good position. She could tap into her reserves as much as she needed to and she would have two days to recover from the effort.

She hit three sharply angled serves to pull out the game. After the last one, she felt the surge of excitement she had expected to kick in when she had first walked on court. Riding the wave, she reeled off eight straight points to build a quick 3-0 lead. Anke shook off her early nerves and found her game but not before Sinjin took the first set 6-3.

The second set was a reversal of the first. Anke was the one who got off to the fast start as Sinjin, perhaps too relaxed after winning the opening set, let her concentration lapse and dropped serve for the first time in the tournament. Painting the lines with her returns, Anke got an insurance break and pushed her lead to 5-0.

During the changeover, Sinjin tried to decide whether to fight for the set or throw it away and prepare for the third. *Make her serve it out and see what happens*, she said to herself as she toweled off. *Hold your serve and see if she starts to feel it. If she tightens up, you still have a chance to win this set. If she doesn't, at least you'll start the third serving first.*

"Time," the chair umpire said.

Sinjin bounced out of her chair and took the court with her head up and her shoulders back. Her positive body language let Anke—and the crowd—know that she wasn't discouraged by the seemingly insurmountable deficit she faced.

One problem with Anke's game was she didn't put enough thought into constructing a point. Her strategy was a simple one: hit every ball as hard as she could. She also rushed through her matches, playing each point as if she were late for dinner. The rules allowed for thirty seconds between points, but she rarely took more than fifteen. Instead of taking some extra time before a big point the way most veterans did, she just grabbed the ball and served.

Common sense said Sinjin should slow the pace in order to throw off Anke's rhythm. Throwing common sense to the wind, she followed Anke's frenetic pace instead of disrupting it. After punching a backhand volley into the open court to hold serve, she sprinted to the baseline to receive Anke's deliveries.

She came in on each of Anke's serves, no matter how good or bad the return. She wanted Anke to feel the pressure of the moment—and from the other side of the net.

Anke missed her first passing shot by an inch then started to press. Her next shot caught the top of the tape. The next two found the middle of the net.

Down 2-5, Sinjin sprinted to her chair for the changeover. Once more, she returned to the court before the end of the allotted ninety seconds. She took half her normal amount of time between points as she quickly held serve for 3-5. Another break and she would be back on track.

"Come on, come on, come on," she chanted to herself.

She won the first point by hitting an unexpected drop shot in the middle of a long rally. On the second, she sliced a backhand return. The ball landed short and stayed low, drawing Anke to the net just as she had intended. Anke got to the ball in plenty of time only to watch Sinjin hit a lob over her head for a clean winner. Love-30.

Continuing to go for broke, Sinjin grabbed the next two points to break serve.

The crowd, dead silent only minutes before, regained its voice.

Sinjin breathed a sigh of relief but reminded herself not to take her foot off the gas. "You're not out of it yet."

When play resumed, she took something off the ball, forcing Anke to generate her own pace. Like a batter who expected a fastball but received a changeup, Anke mistimed her swing. She caught a couple of balls late and overhit the rest. Spraying errors all over the court, she allowed Sinjin to pull even at 5-all.

Two games away from the match, Sinjin finally slowed down. She played at the pace of the server as the rules dictated, but she also made sure Anke had plenty of time to think. Time to rue her missed opportunity.

Anke took deep, gulping breaths to settle her frayed nerves, but the damage was done. Sinjin had her teeth in the match and refused to let go. Playing power tennis from the baseline, she beat Anke at her own game.

She broke Anke at love and served for the match.

When Anke stroked a backhand return long on match point, Sinjin dropped her racquet and raised her hands to her head in disbelief. She had overcome a crisis of confidence in the first set, then she had reeled off seven straight games to win the second.

Anke's eyes were wet when she and Sinjin shook hands at the net. Having been in Anke's position many times before, Sinjin knew Anke wanted to get off the court as fast as possible so she could cry in the locker room, but she had to impart something to her first.

"Experience got me through this one. You're only going to get better. Learn from this."

"I will," Anke said, choking back the tears that were threatening to fall.

Though Anke was distraught over the loss, Sinjin knew she would take her advice to heart. Anke was a hard worker dedicated to improving her game. As soon as she fulfilled her obligations to the press, she would probably head to the practice court to work on the shots Sinjin had pressured her into missing.

Sinjin raised her arms over her head to applaud the cheering crowd. She kept telling herself to act like she had been there before, but she couldn't because she hadn't.

For the first time in her career, she had made it to the second week of Wimbledon.

MIDDLE SUNDAY

Unlike Chandler Freeman, whose off-court activities continued to make headlines, Sinjin's weekend was a quiet one. Though Friday's match had not been physically demanding, it had exacted an emotional toll.

She spent most of Saturday paying the price. While she watched Laure cruise to an easy straight set third round win, she struggled with the realization that the first week of the tournament, as difficult as it had been, was actually the easy part. Now she would have to win four matches in six days. All the round of sixteen matches would be played on Monday. The women's quarterfinals would follow on Tuesday with the semifinals on Thursday and the final on Saturday afternoon. If she kept winning, the condensed schedule would provide a stern test of both her physical and mental endurance.

As the tournament progressed, the matches were bound to get tougher—and longer. The first week, she had tried to win each match in straight sets. The second week, she simply wanted to win each match. She didn't care if the scores were close or one-sided as long as they were in her favor. Her entire career had come down to this. She had one week to prove to herself and to everyone else she belonged on her sport's grandest stage.

In the round of sixteen, she was set to square off against Madeline Harper. Though seeded ninth and ranked ten in the world, the rising star from Ottawa had received very little attention during the first week of the event. Journalists tried to pull interesting quotes from her during her post-match press conferences, but she didn't give much away. She followed the same strategy on court, sacrificing flashiness for workmanlike consistency. But when she spotted an opening, she unleashed a forehand that was as big as anyone's in the game.

To beat her, Sinjin would have to change her tactics yet again. Unlike most baseliners, Madeline made frequent forays to the net, especially on fast surfaces. When they squared off, Sinjin would have to get to the net first and play the baseline well enough to keep Madeline on her heels. But with the match a full twenty-four hours away, she had plenty of time to sit down with Andrew and come up with a game plan. She didn't want to start thinking about Xs and Os just yet. She had something else she needed to do first.

On Middle Sunday, the traditional day of rest during which no matches were played, she took the train to Notting Hill. Outside the tube station, she hailed a cab and directed the driver to a house with a blue door. "Wait for me."

The cab driver tipped his Manchester United cap as if he were a nattily-attired chauffeur. "Yes, Miss Smythe."

Sinjin was still getting used to the star treatment she had been afforded since her upset victory in the first round. She hadn't paid for her own meal or bought her own drink in days. *Funny how a few wins can change everyone's opinion of you. A few days ago, I was a has-been. Now everyone knows my name.*

She climbed out of the backseat and walked up the driveway. Standing on the stoop, she lifted the heavy brass knocker and rapped three times. Laure appeared in the doorway. Sinjin held out her hand, her heart pounding so hard she could feel it thumping against her ribs. She felt like she had just finished a three-hour match when, for all intents and purposes, she was barely halfway through the first set. "Come with me."

Laure glanced at the taxi idling by the curb. "And go where?"

"There's someone I want you to meet."

❖

"Would you like me to wait?" the cabbie asked after Sinjin paid the fare.

"No, we're going to be a while. We'll take the tube back."

"Cheers then," the cabbie said before speeding away.

Laure shoved her hands into the pockets of her cargo shorts. "Should I have packed a lunch?"

"It's not that kind of trip. If you're hungry, I'll take you somewhere when we're done."

Based on Sinjin's much-too-serious expression, Laure doubted she would feel like eating when they were "done."

In contrast to tourist-laden Hyde Park, Hampstead Heath was frequented mostly by locals. On Sunday afternoons, the Heath's three square miles of woods, meadows, hills, ponds, and lakes teemed with residents burning off the calories from lunch or discussing the latest headlines while they basked in the sun.

As she and Sinjin walked through the Heath's open spaces, Laure felt like they had abandoned the city for the country. But then Sinjin led her to a wooden bench perched atop a gently rolling hill and she was treated to a panoramic view of the sprawling metropolis that was London.

"My mother used to bring me and Stephanie here every weekend," Sinjin said, taking a seat. "Just about every momentous event in our lives has taken place here." She patted the spot next to her. "I signed my first professional contract here. Stephanie had her first kiss here."

Squatting in front of the bench, Laure traced her fingers over the initials that had been carved into the wood. SIS. SJS. Sinjin Imogene Smythe. Stephanie Jacinda Smythe. "Where was your first kiss?"

"I haven't had it yet."

"You've probably experienced more first kisses than all my other friends combined."

"I've had kisses that made my toes curl and kisses that made me think twice, but I've never had one where bells ring, angels sing, and I know this is it. Where I know this is the person I'm supposed to spend the rest of my life with. I've never been kissed like that. Have you?"

"Once. You gave it to me."

"Really? When?"

"Three years ago, you kissed me in the middle of Arthur Ashe Stadium. I've never forgotten that moment. Or how I wished it would never end. At the time, I thought I was excited about the title we had just won—and mortified by the fact that twenty thousand people were watching us. Now, the more I think about it, I realize I didn't care about the title or how many people were looking on. I just wanted you to kiss me again."

She took a long look at the bench, finally recognizing it as the one from the photo in Stephanie's foyer. The photo of Sinjin, Stephanie, and their mother that Sinjin rubbed for luck before each match. She felt as if something momentous was about to happen. She sat next to Sinjin, alternating between admiring the view and examining Sinjin's face. Sinjin seemed to be on the verge of tears.

"Who did you want me to meet?" she asked as gently as she could.

"My mum."

Laure must have looked as confused as she felt. Sinjin took her hands in hers.

"In Brighton, we lived close to the pier so we got to see it every day. On the weekends, it was too crowded and too noisy for Mum's taste. She preferred it here. The trip is only an hour by train, but for us, coming to London was like going on holiday. While Stephanie and I ran all over the place getting into everything we could, Mum used to sit here and do crossword puzzles. It's how she improved her English. She would bring *The Times* and a crossword puzzle dictionary and spend hours filling in all the spaces. We weren't allowed to leave until she finished the puzzle of the day. So no matter how long it took, we were here for the duration."

Laure looked out at the Heath. Sinjin's words were so vivid she could clearly see the images she described. She could hear Stephanie and Sinjin giggling while they played. She could see their mother's proud smile as she watched over them.

Sinjin's voice shook as she related the story. She didn't talk about her mother often. Until a couple of nights ago, she had never offered anything other than the most basic information about either of her parents. Even though her mother had been gone for years, she obviously still grieved her loss. She pulled a photo out of her pocket.

Laure looked at the creased picture. Sinjin's mother was an arresting woman with regal bearing, warm brown eyes, and skin the color of dark chocolate. Sinjin and Stephanie looked like the woman in the picture, but their height, caramel complexions, and hazel eyes were signs of their father's contributions to their gene pool.

"When she died, we spread half her ashes in Lagos and the rest here because this was her favorite spot in the whole world. I can still feel her here, so whenever I'm in London, I always come here to sit and talk to her for a while. I brought you here because I wanted her to meet you."

Laure placed a hand over her heart. No one—friend or lover—had ever made such a magnanimous gesture on her behalf. A light breeze bearing a faint scent of coconuts gently kissed her tear-streaked cheeks.

"Coconut rice was Mum's favorite dish. She could eat it three times a day," Sinjin said as the aroma grew stronger. She put her arm around Laure's shoulders and held her tight. "I think she likes you." She pressed a kiss to Laure's temple. "I think I do, too."

ROUND OF SIXTEEN

The second Monday of the tournament brought something none of the organizers wanted to see: rain.

Thanks to a multimillion-dollar translucent roof, the matches on Centre Court could be played until conclusion after a brief delay, but the players on the surrounding courts would have to wait for the downpour to end before they could see action, and even then they weren't guaranteed they would be able to complete their matches. Sinjin was one of those players.

Waiting anxiously in the players' lounge, she peered out at the gunmetal gray sky. Her match was the third one on the schedule for Court Fourteen. If either of the matches preceding hers ran long, she would run the risk of having her match suspended because of darkness. If that happened, it would contract her compact schedule even more. Instead of playing four times in six days with a day off after the quarterfinals, she would have to play for four straight days and she wouldn't have a day off until Friday—if the rain didn't disrupt the rest of the week's schedule.

Wimbledon, like the French Open, did not have lighted courts. Matches at the Australian Open and the U.S. Open were often contested until the wee hours of the morning, but play in Paris and London ended as soon as darkness descended. On normal days, matches at Wimbledon could be played until nearly ten p.m. But with the sun nowhere to be seen, fourth round matches would probably be called at least an hour before then. Centre Court could be bathed in bright artificial light if the need arose, but because the organizers were determined to have the tournament remain a daytime, outdoor event, the lights were illuminated only when inclement weather necessitated the roof's closure.

Sinjin tried to convince herself that if she kept winning, the schedule makers would have no choice but to place her match on Centre Court. Until then, she kept being relegated to the outer courts as the top seeds hogged the spotlight. There had been some upsets in the first week of the tournament, but the top eight seeds were still around, the only exception being her dismissal of Rosana de los Santos in the opening round. Though she was let down by the scheduling committee's decision to place her match on an outer court, she couldn't blame the organizers for not putting her on one of the show courts. Her past results certainly hadn't warranted the exposure. But the way she was playing, the past didn't matter.

Laure scrolled down the Web page displayed on her phone. "According to most forecasts, this front's going to clear out in about an hour, but there may be intermittent showers later this afternoon."

"Fantastic," Sinjin said sarcastically. Each year she told herself the rain affected everyone equally, but each year she could only focus on how it affected her. She had practiced for an hour on one of the indoor courts under Andrew's watchful eye, but the only thing she could do now was wait for the rain to stop. Of all the things she did well, waiting wasn't one of them. Stephanie could watch paint dry and be perfectly content, but Sinjin was more like their father: eager to make things happen.

She paced the perimeter of the players' lounge like a caged tiger.

"Why don't you sit down before you wear a hole in the carpet?" Laure said after she completed another circuit of the room.

She reluctantly complied with Laure's request. She wasn't the only player having problems corralling her nervous energy. All the competitors who hadn't been lucky enough to be scheduled to play on Centre Court were scattered around the lounge. Some played cards, others board or computer games. Some slept, others lined up to take their turns on the Ping-Pong table. A few stood in front of the plasma TV in the corner watching what little live action that was taking place.

On the screen, Blake Freeman was making five-time champion Venus Williams look ordinary. If she got past Madeline Harper, Sinjin would be next on Blake's radar. Most players feared matching up with Blake on her favorite surface in her favorite tournament, but Sinjin was looking forward to the challenge. She wanted a chance to measure herself against the best. And if it happened, she knew the match would be guaranteed to take place on Centre Court. She would finally get her chance to play on the most revered court in her sport. The mere thought of it gave her goose bumps.

When Blake stretched her lead to 6-1, 4-1, Laure rose from her seat. She was scheduled to play the next match on Centre Court. The way Blake was sprinting to the finish line, her match would begin in a matter of minutes.

When she took the court, Laure would be across the net from Maria Sharapova, the Russian glamour girl who had finally found her footing after losing seven months of her career to a shoulder injury. Maria's comeback was nearly complete. Since her return to the tour, she had made the final of one Grand Slam and the semis of two more. She had retooled her service motion, eliminating the double faults that had plagued her game for the past two years. Her fearsome ground strokes were as punishing as ever. All that was missing was another Grand Slam title to add to her already impressive résumé. Laure would have to be on top of her game in order to beat her.

"Good luck."

"Thanks. I'll need it." Laure seemed unwilling to leave. "I won't be able to watch you play today," she said after a moment's hesitation. "Not in person, anyway. I want to, but I can't risk getting sick sitting in the damp air."

Though she understood the reasoning behind Laure's decision, Sinjin was disappointed nevertheless. When Laure was in the stands for her matches, she felt like she was playing to an audience of one. She'd hit a great shot and immediately look at Laure to see her reaction.

Unable to sit still after Laure left, she popped out of her seat and resumed her pacing.

The day was cold and damp. The kind of weather England was famous for. The kind of weather Sinjin had hoped to avoid. Her left knee was talking to her, and she didn't like the things it was saying. She couldn't chase down every shot. Not today. Not unless she wanted to risk injury by taking a tumble on the wet grass.

"Use your head, not your legs," Andrew had advised her during their practice session. "Play all out, but play within yourself. Be smart. Tennis isn't rocket science. You know what you have to do."

Sinjin had answered the question he had left unspoken. "Win the last point."

❖

Laure tried to banish thoughts of Sinjin from her mind. With a formidable opponent across the net, she had enough on her plate without worrying about whether Sinjin would be able to play today. She had to stay focused and maintain her concentration no matter what happened on the other side of the draw. Or in the newspapers.

A knot had formed in her gut when she read the morning's tabloids. Her face was all over the front page. Grainy, long-distance photos of her and Sinjin's emotional visit to Hampstead Heath were everywhere. "Are They or Aren't They?" one headline asked. "Just Friends?" another wanted to know.

By the time she made it to her post-match press conference, it would be like her first Wimbledon all over again, when her run to the final had been overshadowed by the controversy over her sexuality. Sure, the tour's handlers would probably ask the press to limit their queries to her on-court activities, but she knew the moratorium wouldn't last long. If at all. Having her face splashed on the front page of every newspaper from here to Timbuktu wasn't her thing. She liked flying under the radar, quietly going about her business and garnering very little attention until championship weekend when the focus was squarely on her game, not her personal life. So much for that.

She lost the first three games of her round of sixteen match while her head was in a fog. She broke Maria to get back on serve in the first set, then broke again to take the lead. She won the first set 6-4 and ran through the second 6-1.

She was playing better with each round. She could feel her game start to come together. If she peaked at the right time and kept her lapses in concentration to a minimum, the title was hers for the taking. Claiming Sinjin's heart would have to wait.

❖

Two more games. That was all she needed. Sinjin looked up at the darkening sky. Did she have enough time? Madeline had slowed the pace in the past few games, trying to drag things out. She was obviously hoping for a continuation. Sinjin was determined not to give her one. A late break had earned her the first set; an early one had given her the lead in the second.

Keeping the points short, she played exclusively serve-and-volley in her next service game to pull ahead 5-3. One more game. If she broke serve, the match was over.

Even though her back was to the wall, Madeline refused to give in. She fought her way out of a 0-30 hole to hold serve and pull to within a game. Then she spent the entire changeover attempting to convince the chair umpire to call the match.

"It's so dark out here I can barely see my hand in front of my face," she said while the crowd whistled in displeasure. "What do you want us to do, play by moonlight? If you expect us to do that, you'd better round up some balls that glow in the dark."

The chair umpire called the tournament referee for advice.

Sinjin's heart sank when the official reached for his walkie-talkie. She wanted to play the next day, but in the quarterfinals, not the round of sixteen.

The chair umpire lowered the volume on his two-way radio and signaled for both players to join him. The overflow crowd strained to hear the quiet conversation. "You have one more game. After that, we call the match."

"Why don't we call it now?" Madeline asked.

The chair umpire stood firm. If a match had to be called, officials preferred to do it at a point that didn't favor one player over another. After one more game, the set would end at 6-4 or be knotted at 5-all. "It's only fair."

The crowd roared its approval when the players returned to the court. Standing at the service line, Sinjin did her best to keep her knees from knocking. She had never felt such pressure. Every cliché in the book could be attached to this next game. If she won it, she would join the Last Eight Club. If she lost it, all bets were off.

Two sloppy volleys put her in a hole.

"Fifteen-thirty," the chair umpire said.

Slow down. Sinjin reminded herself to play one point at a time. Though she wanted to get the game in before darkness fell, doing so would be pointless if she let the game slip through her fingers.

Picking on Madeline's suspect backhand, she tossed a serve out wide and followed it to the net. Madeline's return was better than she expected, but she picked it off her shoe tops for a drop volley winner.

Thirty-all.

She reached match point with an ace down the middle, then promptly squandered it by blowing a forehand volley.

When the crowd groaned in disappointment, Sinjin resisted the urge to hang her head.

It was just one point. You've got to play at least two more.

Granted new life, Madeline took advantage of her second chance. She smacked a blistering forehand passing shot to reach break point. The crowd groaned even louder and Sinjin's shoulders slumped for the first time all tournament.

Sinjin slowly picked herself off the ground. Her diving effort to reach Madeline's forehand had come up just short. Would she do the same?

This is your chance, she thought as anger replaced her nerves. *This is your moment. Don't throw it away.*

Her clothes were covered in grass stains, but she paid them no mind. When the ball boy offered her a towel, she waved him away.

It was time to get dirty.

Her eleventh ace brought her to deuce. Her twelfth to match point.

She waited for the ball boy to toss her the ball she had used to serve the previous point. *This is the one*, she thought, giving the ball a fervent kiss. *Let's end this*.

The serve felt pure when it left her racquet. For a split-second, she thought she had hit another ace. Evoking vintage Jimmy Connors, Madeline threw herself at the return and somehow managed to get her racquet on it. Sinjin stretched her eyes wide to see clearly in the fading light while she raced to the net to intercept the weak return. When she drew her racquet back, the crowd murmured in anticipation. She smashed the ball into the open court. It landed well out of Madeline's reach and bounced into the stands. She sank to her knees as the crowd leaped to its feet.

"Game, set, match, Miss Smythe," the chair umpire said. "Miss Smythe wins two sets to love. Six-three, six-four."

❖

After they completed their respective press conferences, Laure and Sinjin headed to Notting Hill. Sinjin slumped on the couch, seemingly too tired to string two sentences together let alone take advantage of the fact they were alone for the first time in days. Carrying a nation's hopes and dreams on your shoulders was exhausting. Laure had carried the same weight for years. When she had finally relieved herself of her burden by winning the French Open a few weeks prior, she had felt lighter than air. She hoped Sinjin would experience the same sense of euphoria one day. But not this year. This year was her time.

"You never said it would be this hard," Sinjin said. "Winning a tournament is tough, but this is like winning two or three of them. The second week, the matchups in each round are worthy of a final. And that"—she pointed to her cell phone, which was vibrating almost nonstop on the table—"*that* is driving me crazy. Companies are coming out of the woodwork, all wanting to know if I'll endorse their products. Even my old clothing company has come courting. They offered me a signing bonus and a lucrative extension if I agreed to let them reinstate my deal."

"What did you say?"

"Thanks but no thanks. Only I wasn't nearly that polite. If I'm worthy of such fantastic offers now, why wasn't I four months ago?"

Sinjin's voice was tinged with anger. Laure couldn't blame her for having a chip on her shoulder, but now wasn't the time to seek retribution for real or imagined slights. She tried to smooth her ruffled feathers.

"It's not you who has changed. It's the size of your audience. You're a hot commodity now and will be for a while. Don't be stubborn. This is your chance to secure your financial future. The trickle of calls you're getting now won't compare to the flood you'll receive when we make it to Saturday's final."

Sinjin frowned. "You talk about the two of us playing for the title as if it's a done deal. Have you taken a look at the draw sheet?"

In the next round, Sinjin would play Blake in the showcase match on Centre Court. Their opening act? Viktoriya against Serena Williams in a battle of current and former world number ones. The matches scheduled for Court One weren't too shabby, either. Laure would open play by taking on Mirjana Petkovic, a hard-hitting Serbian teenager bidding to become her relatively new nation's third Grand Slam champion. Then third-ranked Chandler Freeman would square off against the resurgent Kim Clijsters.

"I know we have formidable opponents in our way, players who are playing as well as we are, if not better, but what we've been dreaming about for weeks is close to becoming a reality. I've never lost to Mirjana and I have a good record against Viktoriya. I've beaten her here before and I know I can do it again. On your side of the draw, the Freeman sisters aren't going to be easy, but Blake's injured and Chandler hasn't won the title in three years. This is the only tournament where she consistently runs into players who believe they can beat her even when she's playing her A-game. Blake has beaten her here three times, I've done it twice, and Maria

Sharapova has done it once. Thursday, you could add your name to the list. Pretend it's Miami all over again. Would that help?"

The ten-day hard court tournament in Miami was considered the tour's fifth major. The last time she had qualified for the event in her adopted hometown, Sinjin had upset Chandler in the third round.

"In Miami, I beat Chandler and lost to Blake. I don't want to lose. To anyone."

Laure stroked Sinjin's furrowed brow. Sinjin had been irritable all day. At first Laure had attributed her unease to the weather. Now she feared something else might be the cause. Was the stress of the tournament or the uncertainty of a new relationship to blame?

"Let's stop worrying about wins and losses and enjoy our time together. My parents are having dinner in town tonight. Stephanie and Nicolas are off doing who knows what. Gabrielle and Kendall are off doing who knows who. Why don't we stay in instead of going out to dinner?"

"Because it feels like the walls are closing in and I need to get out of here. I need to breathe."

Laure remembered the moment of panic she'd faced when she neared her first Grand Slam title. When everything she had worked so hard to achieve was just a few steps away. So near and yet so far.

"Let's go out," Sinjin said. "There's a table at Fog with our names on it."

Laure shook her head. "We have matches to play tomorrow. I don't want to trek all the way into town, wait an hour for our food, then spend another two hours trying to extricate you from the clutches of your adoring public."

Sinjin cocked her head as if seeing the world from a different angle would help her see things more clearly. "Or is there another reason you want to hide out behind closed doors? It's the press attention, isn't it? You can't afford to be seen with me."

If Sinjin had aimed the verbal arrow at her heart, she had certainly hit her mark.

"I don't like being the subject of speculation, but—"

"Is that code for you can't make headlines without losing your focus?"

Laure tried to keep her voice level despite the anxiety rising inside her like a flood-swollen river. "As long as we know what's really going on between us, it doesn't matter what anyone else thinks. Or writes."

"What's really going on between us? I'd love for you to define it for me. We hang out every night, you flirt just enough to convince me you're interested, then you put on the brakes whenever I make a move, and you send me home with a serious case of blue balls. If what other people said about us didn't matter, you wouldn't have waved that tabloid in my face last week when Kendall and I were on the front page."

Laure backed off as the conversation took an unexpected turn. She didn't want to start a fight, even though Sinjin seemed to be itching for one. "I think the pressure's making you paranoid."

"No, the pressure's helping me see things clearly." Sinjin pushed herself off the couch. "I don't know what I was thinking. The middle of a Grand Slam event isn't the time to even think about a relationship, let alone embark on one. We should cut our losses and call it a day."

"I thought you said the time for excuses was over."

Laure's words stopped Sinjin in her tracks.

"If you walk out that door," Laure said, "that tells me you didn't mean any of the things you've been saying the past few months. That tells me you don't believe in yourself or your game. Do you expect me to believe everything you said in Hampstead Heath was just a line? I was there. I know better. But if you want to take the easy way out, go ahead."

Sinjin reached for the doorknob.

"Say hello to Abby for me," Laure said. "Or whoever you happen to pick up on the way home."

Sinjin whirled to face her. "I'm not that person anymore."

"Are you sure? From this perspective, it still looks like you're running away at the first sign of adversity. The second this relationship stopped being fun, you decided to do what you do best—avoid the heavy lifting and take the easy way out. If Blake puts up a fight, are you going to tank your match tomorrow, too?"

Sinjin didn't respond.

"How many times are you going to do this to yourself?" Laure asked. "How many times are you going to let yourself get close to what you want, then get scared and shrink from the challenge?"

Sinjin still didn't say anything. Her face was a blank mask. Laure had seen that look before. She had seen it on Sinjin's face every time she lost a match she should have won. Every time she convinced herself she was second best.

"If you want to beat Blake tomorrow," Laure said, "I can tell you how to do it. If you want to be with me, you're going to have to figure that out on your own."

QUARTERFINALS

A crowd shadowed Sinjin during the long walk from the locker room to Aorangi Park. She signed whatever was thrust in front of her and blindly returned it without interacting with the object's owner. The crowd grew bigger with each step. By the time she reached the practice courts, she felt claustrophobic.

She'd barely slept since she left Laure's last night. The scene they'd acted out kept running through her head.

Last night she'd had a choice to make. She had to decide which was more important, winning Wimbledon or winning Laure's heart. She'd chosen the former.

Holding her racquet over her head, she stretched to her left then to her right. She groaned pleasurably when her back gave a satisfying pop. She was so close to getting everything she had ever wanted. So close to getting a second chance. A Grand Slam title was within reach. Laure had already won four majors. Laure could take time to stop and smell the roses. She couldn't. Not if she wanted to get where Laure had already been.

She and Laure had seen each other almost every other day for weeks. The last few had seen them start to develop something special. Something real. Too real. She hadn't gone to Laure's last night intending to end their courtship, but it was the right thing to do.

Being with Laure was easy in the beginning when the championship match was so far away. The closer it came—the closer they crept to playing each other in a final both hungered to win—the harder it got for her to spend so much time with Laure in a casual setting. How was she supposed to look across the net on Saturday and see an opponent instead of a woman she had begun to care for? Laure might be able to compartmentalize her feelings, but she couldn't.

Last night it had come to a head. Last night Laure was probably trying to be helpful, but she had reminded Sinjin too much of Viktoriya. Trying to control her in ways both subtle and overt. She had felt herself falling into a familiar trap. One Viktoriya had set time and time again. Her gut told her Laure wouldn't resort to such tricks, but her head said the opposite. She had listened to her head—and she had been second-guessing herself ever since.

Every time she began to doubt her decision, she remembered her slide down the rankings and the underhanded comments from Viktoriya that had precipitated it. She couldn't let herself get that close to another player again. Not now. Not ever.

Despite her efforts to push Laure away, all she wanted to do when she saw her approach the practice court was pull her closer.

Laure greeted Andrew with a warm hug, but her greeting for Sinjin was decidedly frostier. "Good morning," Laure said, studiously avoiding meeting her eye. "I'll take that end." She took off her warm-up jacket and jogged to the far side of the court.

"New practice partner?" Andrew asked after Laure was out of earshot.

"Something like that."

Andrew extinguished his cigarette on the sole of his shoe as he watched Laure skip along the baseline to warm up her legs. Gabrielle led her through her paces. Nicolas observed them from a few feet away.

"I would be remiss if I didn't take the opportunity to remind you this is no time for distractions," Andrew said. "Front page photos of you snogging Laure Fortescue qualify as distractions, don't you think?"

"A kiss on the cheek hardly qualifies as snogging. After last night, I don't think I have to worry about a repeat performance."

"Then what is she doing here?"

Proving that I was right about her. She is *better than I deserve.*

"She knows what it feels like to defeat Blake Freeman. I want to be able to say the same."

"Wouldn't we all?"

Players weren't the only ones who felt pressure. Coaches did, too. Everything from their tactics to their training methods to their motivational strategies could be and often were called into question. The constant second-guessing had hastened Andrew's exit from the sport ten years ago. He was back, but Sinjin didn't know for how long. He had volunteered to help her for one tournament, no more. If she wanted him to help her finish the rest of the year, would he be up to the challenge? Up to it? Yes. Willing? That was another story. In the back of his mind, he was probably looking forward to his re-retirement. Life was so much easier without the eyes of the world upon you.

"When Andy Murray lost in the final of the Aussie Open the year he seemed destined to claim his first Grand Slam title, I told myself I wouldn't see another UK native win a major in this lifetime," Andrew said. "Now you're only three matches away from proving me wrong."

He rubbed his stubbled chin as they watched Blake warm up on a nearby court. Blake was a supreme athlete and superb tactician, about as complete a player as Sinjin had ever seen. Sure, Blake had weaknesses, but she was so fast on her feet and so strong off the ground most of her opponents were unable to expose her shortcomings. Laure was one of the rare few. And, despite the uncertainty that surrounded their personal relationship, she was willing to help Sinjin join her ranks.

"You're right," Andrew said. "A good coach is one who isn't afraid to solicit outside opinions upon occasion. For you to be successful, my voice doesn't have to be the only one in your ear. Let's hear what she has to say."

Sinjin and Andrew joined Laure and Nicolas at the net. Together, they laid out the strategy Sinjin hoped would propel her to the biggest win of her career.

❖

On paper, Laure had the easiest of the four quarterfinal matches. But matches weren't played on paper. Her opponent was one of the hardest hitters on the tour, and she had bashed her way through four quality players to reach the last eight. Laure couldn't afford to take her lightly.

She closed her eyes and began her mental preparations for the upcoming match. Employing the techniques her sports psychologist had taught her, she visualized the match from start to finish. From the first point to match point. Then she did it again. Each time, she saw herself coming out on top.

"You're getting sloppy."

Laure opened her eyes to find Viktoriya standing in front of her. Viktoriya's tuxedo-inspired tennis dress was fashionable enough to go straight from the court to a night on the town.

"Excuse me?"

Viktoriya tossed a day-old tabloid into Laure's lap. Laure glanced at the newspaper but quickly turned away. The series of photographs on the front page depicted her and Sinjin crying on the bench in Hampstead Heath. The headline above the photo read, "Lovers' Tiff." The moment she and Sinjin had shared on Sunday had been incredibly beautiful. Nothing could cheapen the experience. Not what transpired between them last night or Viktoriya's antics now.

"Aren't you the one who said 'headlines should be used to describe what I do on the court, not who I do off of it'?"

"I'm not 'doing' Sinjin," Laure said through clenched teeth. "Not that it's any of your business."

She stood and tried to brush past, but Viktoriya stood her ground. "If Mirjana doesn't beat you today, I will. As for Sinjin, leave her to me. Think how painful it would be for her to get all the way to the finals and lose. You're too soft to knock her off. I won't have that problem. See you in the semifinals."

Laure resisted the urge to chase after Viktoriya and wipe the cruel smile off her beautiful face. She clenched and unclenched her fists as she tried to regain control of her emotions. Some players drew fuel from their anger, their fury inspiring them to play better.

She always played worse, her level of play declining as her blood pressure rose.

If she didn't get centered—and soon—her tournament could be over.

❖

Sinjin did some of her best thinking in the shower, one of the few places she could completely clear her head and focus on what was most important. She thought she could probably solve most of the world's problems if she remained in her makeshift sensory deprivation chamber long enough. At the moment, the task at hand was solving the puzzle that was Blake Freeman.

She let the warm spray wash over her as she attempted to absorb the information Laure had imparted during their practice session that morning. Laure had been full of advice but none of the expected variety. Sinjin had expected her to share technical tips like where she should place her serve or if she should aim for Blake's forehand or backhand side on an important point. Instead, Laure's advice had been purely psychological.

"Blake's presence is so intimidating she wins half her matches simply by walking out of the locker room. You have to show her from the beginning—even before the coin toss—that you feel like you belong on the same court with her. Then you have to draw a line in the sand. Pick a part of the court and make it yours. For me, it's the baseline. For you, it should be the net. The net is yours. It belongs to you. Don't let Blake take it away from you. Defend it to the death if you have to. Not literally, but you get the idea."

Laure's closing comment had been well thought out, its Zen-like minimalism so soothing it immediately erased Sinjin's fears about the match. "At this level, it's all about execution. Blake knows what you're going to do and you know what she's going to do. Whoever does it better will win. It's as simple as that."

And it was that simple. Blake was going to play her game and Sinjin was going to play hers. Whoever did it better would book a spot in the final four.

She turned off the water and reached for a towel. After drying off, she returned to the locker room. The cavernous room was empty and eerily quiet. With most of the unseeded players knocked out of the event, she had the room to herself. Mirjana Petkovic was the only other unseeded player left in the women's draw, and with Laure up a set and 5-1, Mirjana's tournament was rapidly coming to an end.

On Centre Court, Serena Williams was fighting her heart out, but she was still hampered by a foot injury that had kept her out of the game for months. Exploiting Serena's limited mobility, Viktoriya won the first set 6-2 and had forged ahead 4-0 in the second. Serena was tenacious enough to come back, but Viktoriya was such a good front-runner Sinjin didn't expect her to let up until the match was over. If then. Her number one ranking was on the line. She needed to win to keep pace with Blake. To stay ahead of her.

When they were teenagers, becoming number one was all Viktoriya talked about. She had made it to the top of the mountain, but she was on the verge of falling off her perch. Unless Sinjin beat Blake in the next round. Then Viktoriya would be safe. And she would have Sinjin to thank. Sinjin intended to do her part. She longed to see Viktoriya taken down a notch, but part of her wanted to do the job herself. In a couple of days, the pleasure could be Laure's. If Laure and Viktoriya squared off on Thursday, who would she root for? Would she be driven by loyalty or her unquenched thirst for revenge?

"If you don't beat Blake, none of it will matter. So get your head out of your arse and take her down."

After her match, Laure snarled in disgust as she tossed her wet towel in the receptacle outside the shower stall. She had won easily to advance to the semifinals, which meant she was now free to focus on what she wanted to put out of her mind: Sinjin. Was pursuing a relationship with her worth the heartache she encountered on the way?

She wrapped a dry towel around her body and headed to the locker room. Blake Freeman had been assigned the cubicle next to hers. Her sister Chandler had the one on the other side. As they did before most matches—except when they were playing each other—the sisters sat side-by-side comparing notes on each other's next opponents.

Laure squeezed between them to get to her locker. "Excuse me," she said, apologizing for interrupting the impromptu coaching session.

The sisters ceased their whispered conversation. After Laure pulled her sports bra over her head, she turned to find two sets of aquamarine eyes staring at her.

Chandler broke the silence.

"Are you going to tell her or am I going to have to do it?"

"Tell who what?"

Chandler pursed her lips. "Come on, Laure. Don't play dumb. You know what I'm talking about. Are you going to tell Sinjin what Viktoriya said?"

Laure continued getting dressed. "If Viktoriya has messages she wants to deliver, she can deliver them herself."

"Sinjin deserves to know, don't you think?"

"Know what? That Viktoriya's willing to do and say anything to hold on to her ranking? I think she's fully aware of that fact, thanks."

Chandler tossed her racquet bag over her shoulder. "Suit yourself." She bumped knuckles with her sister. "See you on the other side."

Chandler headed to Court One. Blake, the older and more introspective one, stayed behind. "Are you okay?" she asked, resting a consoling hand on Laure's arm.

Laure nodded, but touched by Blake's obvious concern for her, couldn't speak.

"I know it's not in your nature, Laure, but sometimes you have to fight for what you want. To get back at Viktoriya, you have to beat her at her own game. Not the one between the lines. The one between the ears." Blake tapped her temples.

"Thanks, Blake. I would say, 'Good luck,' but—"

Blake chuckled. "Yeah, I know."

After Blake left, Laure sat in front of her locker and tried to pull herself together. She was always on edge during a major but not like this. Never like this. She didn't know whether to laugh or cry. Both felt appropriate somehow. How funny was it that she thought she and Sinjin could lay their respective baggage aside and start fresh with each other? And how sad that they couldn't.

❖

Sinjin headed to the holding area to wait to be called to the court. The room, filled with glass display cases and wood-paneled accents, was worthy of a museum exhibit. She examined the photos of current and former champions while she slowly stretched her arms, legs, and back.

"I see you decided to go with the shorts today."

Sinjin turned to face Blake Freeman. "I wanted to be able to keep up with you." She hoped the sartorial change of pace would result in a change of luck. She had never played her best tennis against Blake. Not even close. She couldn't allow that trend to continue. Such a desultory effort wasn't worthy of Centre Court, the site of some of the greatest matches that had ever been played.

Blake cocked her head, a quizzical look on her face. She and Sinjin had been competing against each other for years, but Blake narrowed her eyes as if she were encountering Sinjin for the first time. In a way, she was. She had never faced *this* Sinjin before.

This is it. This is when she normally gets me. When she sizes me up and I come up short.

Sinjin coolly returned Blake's gaze. "How's the wrist?" she asked casually. Though heavily taped, Blake's injured right wrist hadn't hampered her play. Her booming serve had lost none of its sting. Her game had been so impressive some of the players she had beaten wondered aloud if she were actually hurt.

Blake flinched at the non sequitur. Her probe for potential weaknesses had come up empty, but Sinjin's seemed to have hit the bull's-eye.

"It's as good as new." Blake held up her arm and performed a close approximation of a royal wave.

Despite Blake's insistence that her wrist wasn't a cause for concern, Sinjin noticed that when she bent to pick up her racquet bag, she made sure to use her left hand instead of her right. That was the moment Sinjin knew she was going to win. Her game plan was perfect. Her opponent was less than a hundred percent. How could she lose?

❖

Laure watched from the players' lounge as Blake and Sinjin went through the ten-minute warm-up. Only in tennis did players help their opponents practice shots that could later be used to defeat them.

Sinjin missed nearly all of her practice serves, but Laure paid that no heed. Lots of players were awful in warm-ups but went on to play great once the match started. Laure chose to examine their body language instead. Which woman was brimming with confidence and which one was only faking it?

Blake had made so many appearances on Centre Court she had come to refer to the place as her personal playground. Playing yet another match there was no big deal for her. Sinjin, as had been widely reported, had never set foot on the court. When she finally walked onto it for the first time, she had been as saucer-eyed as a Hummel figurine, her lips clearly forming the word "wow."

Despite her struggles during the warm-up, Sinjin seemed completely at ease when the match began. She improved on the form that had carried her to the quarterfinals while Blake's wondrous game abandoned her.

"They're playing as if their rankings are reversed," Gabrielle said. "Sinjin's the one making all the shots. Blake's the one making all the errors."

"Blake certainly picked the wrong time to come up small in a big match. I wonder if Sinjin will play as well the rest of the year as she has the past two weeks," Laure replied.

"If she wins the tournament, it won't matter. She'll be a millionaire a hundred times over and she'll have more endorsements than you could shake a stick at. Even if she never won another match, she'd be set for life."

Laure rested her chin on the heel of her hand as she watched Sinjin aim another serve at Blake's body. Safe but effective, the ploy had worked time and time again. Blake's normally lethal return game had been nullified. Her ground game had been tamed, too. Sinjin didn't give Blake anything to work with. Instead of going for the lines, she directed most of her shots down the middle of the court, taking away Blake's ability to craft the acutely angled passing shots she was known for.

Blake hit the occasional winner, but they were few and far between. Sinjin raced to an early lead and never looked back. In a little over an hour, she found herself serving for the match at 6-3, 5-2.

The Centre Court crowd, which had greeted each error from Blake's racquet with stunned silence, began to buzz with anticipation.

Some players liked to draw crowds into the action on court in order to feed off their energy. Sinjin used to be one of those players. In her previous incarnation, she tried so hard to entertain the fans she forgot to give them what they wanted to see even more than trick shots or percussive serves: a win. In the Wimbledon quarterfinals for the first time, she played with blinders on, concentrating solely on her opponent. Except for the occasional glance to the Friends Box for reassurance, she kept her focus on the match.

She stepped up to the service line a game away from victory. Four quick points later, she was through to a Grand Slam semifinal for the first time in three years. The crowd, though ecstatic over her win, gave Blake a respectful ovation.

Despite her obvious disappointment, Blake was gracious in defeat. "You played like a champion out there today," she said when she and Sinjin shook hands at the net. "Keep it up and you might become one."

"Thanks, B."

After shaking hands with the chair umpire, Sinjin raised her racquet over her head to salute the crowd. Their full-throated roar gave her goose bumps.

Moments like this were why she had become a tennis player. This was why she had left home at fifteen. This was why she had spent so many hours on the practice court. This was why she trained so intensely. This was why she had kept going even when she wanted to stop. This was why she and Stephanie had sacrificed their present to bet on a better future. Her future had arrived.

But she couldn't dwell on what had just happened. She had to start thinking ahead. In the next round, she would face not one player but two.

She spent her post-match shower trying to formulate a game plan.

The Freeman sisters were never far apart when they played a Grand Slam event, one observing while the other played. Though their parents were their official coaches, they usually turned to each other for advice. When she played Chandler in the semifinals, Sinjin knew Blake would be watching from the Friends Box after telling Chandler what to expect. The game plan that had worked so well against Blake would be useless against Chandler. If Sinjin tried to employ the same tactics, Chandler would be ready for them.

In the semis, Sinjin would have to play the match of her life. Again.

She turned off the water and reached for the towel she had hung on the peg just outside the shower stall. She came up empty. She sluiced water off her face with her hands. She looked down, thinking the towel had fallen to the floor. It wasn't there either.

"Looking for this?" Viktoriya held the towel just out of reach.

Sinjin jerked her thumb toward the door. "The seeded players' locker room is that way."

"Don't worry. I won't stay long." Viktoriya tossed her the towel.

Sinjin dried off and quickly began to dress. Most players left little to the imagination in the locker room. She was no different.

She could have a conversation stark naked and think nothing of it. Standing in front of Viktoriya, she felt exposed.

"I just wanted to thank you," Viktoriya said.

"For what?"

Viktoriya's brilliant smile had enough wattage to illuminate all the British Isles. "I'm still number one and I owe it all to you. Now I can relax and play my best tennis."

Viktoriya had barely broken a sweat all tournament. If she hadn't played her best tennis yet, she would be impossible to beat. Or was that what she wanted her to think?

Sinjin freed herself from Viktoriya's clutches. "If you make it past Laure, I'm going to be waiting for you."

Viktoriya roared with laughter. "If that's supposed to be a threat, try again. It sounds more like incentive."

"If you make it past Laure, I'm going to be waiting for you," Sinjin repeated. "And I'm going to beat you."

Viktoriya's smile devolved into a smirk. "For what it's worth, I hope you do win on Thursday. Then one queen will get to watch another."

Viktoriya walked away in apparent triumph. Sinjin let her go. As far as she was concerned, the last word was yet to be uttered. And when it was spoken, she would be the one saying it.

The next day, Laure settled into her seat on the patio. At the All England Club five miles away, the men were playing their quarterfinal matches. The most anticipated match of the day was Andy Murray's showdown against Roger Federer. Murray owned the regal Swiss in tour events but had never beaten him in a Grand Slam tournament. If he was to win his first Wimbledon title, he would have to take down the man who had garnered six of them.

With the men assuming center stage, Laure was grateful for the day off. The break gave her a chance to get some much-needed rest. She was fine physically—thanks to Gabrielle and Kendall, she had never been in better shape—but she was emotionally exhausted.

For most of the past month, she had been on top of the world. When she won the French Open, she didn't think she could get any higher. Then she started to develop a new appreciation for Sinjin Smythe. She had trained with her. Bantered with her. Laughed with her. Cried with her. She had listened to her stories. She had shared her own. Each day, her heart had soared to greater heights. Which made her current low feel that much worse.

She opened her sketchpad, pulled out her charcoal pencil, and began to sketch something suitably dark.

Her cell phone rang. She wiped her hand on her shorts and automatically reached for her phone. Sinjin's mobile number was printed on the display. Laure's thumb hovered over the Answer button. Was Sinjin calling to apologize or pretend nothing had ever happened? Last night or over the past few weeks.

She sent the call to voice mail and returned to her sketch. She kept one eye on the phone until the message indicator began to flash.

"And now for the *coup de grâce*."

She accessed her voice mail and lifted the phone to her ear.

"Are you screening all your calls or just mine?" Sinjin's message began. "Even though it's only been twenty-four hours, I feel like it's been twenty-four days since the last time I talked to you. I almost called you so many times last night. I reached for the phone so often I'll probably develop a hitch in my forehand." A deep sigh, followed by a long pause. "I suppose I should get to the point. I wanted to thank you for everything you've done for me. Yes, I know I've told you before. I'm going to keep telling you until you finally realize how generous you've been. Good luck tomorrow. Maybe, when this is over, you'll let me buy you a drink. I know where I can get a good deal on a bottle of wine. Cheers."

Laure fingered the numbers on the keypad. No matter how much she wanted to remain angry with Sinjin, she couldn't manage the feat. But she couldn't call her back. Not yet. She had two more matches to win first.

She toggled over to her text messages, pulled up Sinjin's number, and typed a short reply.

You're welcome.

❖

Against Andrew's objections, Sinjin had decided to take the day off. What had Laure said in Roehampton?

"Tennis is a big part of my life, but I don't let it consume me. If I wake up and feel like I'd rather spend the day doing something other than chasing after a fuzzy yellow ball, I do. I know coming back is important to you, but you need to find a balance."

Sinjin's drawing skills were so bad she could barely make a stick figure recognizable. She found her balance where she always did. On a bench in Hampstead Heath.

She stretched her legs in front of her and enjoyed the warmth of the late afternoon sun. She raised her face to the sky.

"Almost there, Mum," she whispered. "Almost there."

Her phone buzzed against her hip. She pulled the phone out of its holster. She had two text messages.

The first was a score alert. Andy Murray had just lost to Roger Federer in five grueling sets. Combined with Abby's loss in doubles earlier in the week, that left her as the only player of local interest in the entire tournament. She felt the tremendous weight on her shoulders grow even heavier.

The second message was from Laure.

You're welcome.

She didn't know how to interpret what Laure had written. Was Laure warming up or growing colder?

She slid the phone back into its holster. She might be two matches away from winning Wimbledon, but she might have already lost something much more important.

SEMIFINALS

The match was ninety minutes old, but Laure still hadn't found the range on her serve. Each time she went for the hard, flat one down the middle, she'd hit it just long or into the net. Facing one of the best returners in the sport, she knew she was lucky to be in the match at all, let alone tied at a set apiece. Guile had gotten her this far. Now, with Viktoriya starting to get a better read on her serve, she would have to rely on guts. She needed to sacrifice pace in favor of percentage—and hope like hell her ground game could save the day.

As she grew older, wins—especially Grand Slam wins— became more precious; losses more devastating. She wanted to win this Wimbledon nearly as much as she had wanted to win the French Open. Her win at the French had felt like the culmination of her career. Another win at Wimbledon would remind her of the beginning. The All England Lawn Tennis Club was the site of her first Grand Slam singles title. She had won the Ladies' Plate when she was twenty, claiming the coveted trophy while she was too young and too naïve to realize winning majors was harder than it looked.

Knowing she was in the Wimbledon semifinals for the last time, she had started out anxiously. Facing Viktoriya was a daunting task that required every ounce of her concentration, which had faded in and out during the early rounds. By the time she got locked in during the semis, she had already fallen behind.

She had double faulted twice in the first three points, gifting Viktoriya a break in the opening game of the match. Viktoriya had claimed the first set 6-4, but she had bounced back to win the second set in a tiebreaker. As the third set began, momentum was on her side. So why did she feel like she was holding on by her fingernails?

She looked at the stats as they flashed across the scoreboard. She had more winners than errors and her first serve percentage was a gaudy eighty-five. Both positive signs. But she hadn't come close to breaking Viktoriya's serve. In fact, the break in the first game of the match was the only time either player had dropped serve all day. Each of her service games had been a struggle. Viktoriya had breezed through hers while she had labored to hold.

She tried to look on the bright side. If she could hang on long enough—if she could keep fighting off break points and remain within striking distance—she could pull off the upset. All she needed was a chance. Just one chance.

She glanced at the Friends Box. Viktoriya's team occupied the front row; hers took up the second. Nicolas and Gabrielle sat next to her parents. Stephanie and Kendall rounded out the row. Laure had never felt so supported or so loved. But the person whose support she needed most wasn't there. Sinjin, who was scheduled to play the second semifinal, wasn't there. Not physically, anyway.

Whenever Laure felt herself getting tight, she remembered one of Sinjin's lousy jokes and immediately began to relax. Whenever her spirits started to flag, she could hear Sinjin urging her on like she had in training. And when she finally strung enough points together to break Viktoriya's serve and take a 5-4 lead in the third set, she could almost hear her leading the cheers.

Adrenaline coursed through Laure's body as she sat in her chair during the changeover. She was so close now she could taste it. So could her family and friends. Her parents looked calm, but she could see their excitement—their relief—bubbling just beneath their placid exteriors. The rest of her supporters were more demonstrative. Stephanie and Kendall stood throughout the changeover, clapping rhythmically along with the rest of the crowd. Nicolas and Gabrielle cheered right along with them.

"Stay strong," Nicolas said, shaking his clenched fists. "Serve it out."

Gabrielle raised a finger in the air. "One more game."

Nodding in assent, Laure knew the next game would be one of the hardest she had ever tried to win.

A few days ago, Sinjin wondered who she would root for— Laure or Viktoriya. When Laure hit a gorgeous backhand down the line to take the lead in the third set, she had her answer. And it had nothing to do with match-ups or career head-to-head results. It had nothing to do with loyalty or revenge. She wanted Laure to win because she was in love with her.

"Yes!" she shouted, her voice echoing off the walls.

The locker room attendant covered her mouth with her hand, but not before Sinjin noticed her indulgent smile, the kind of smile mothers reserved for their children who have done something cute but borderline embarrassing. Blushing, Sinjin moved closer to her computer screen. She had said she wouldn't watch the match so she wouldn't expend much-needed emotional energy rooting for or against either player. But hearing the crowd's distant roar without knowing who or what had prompted the sound was even more nerve-wracking than watching the match unfold. She had booted up her laptop near the end of the second set—just in time to see Laure win the pivotal tiebreaker seven points to five. Now Laure was only four points away from the match. Four points away from the finals.

Sinjin wiped her sweaty palms on her pants as she peered at the images on the computer screen. She wished the changeover hadn't disrupted play. Ninety seconds was a long time to think. Especially when tennis history was on the line.

When play resumed, though, Laure looked focused. She looked like she knew what she had to do. But would that be enough? She had a history of blowing winning leads and Viktoriya wasn't going to go down without a fight. In the ensuing battle of wills, who would be declared the victor?

"If you win the first point, the game is yours." Sinjin talked to the computer screen as if Laure could hear her. She hoped she could. "Win the first point, get ahead of her, and the rest is easy. I'll be right behind you. We have a date to keep."

❖

Laure had always been such a crowd favorite at Wimbledon she sometimes felt half-English. As she prepared to serve for the match, she could feel the crowd's apprehension. She could feel how much they wanted her to win. And how afraid they were that she might lose. She felt the same fear.

The first point was crucial. If she won it, she could relax and cruise through the rest of the game. If she lost the game, the match would be even, but momentum would switch to Viktoriya's side of the court.

She went for a hard, flat serve down the T. The serve was the fastest she had ever hit in her life—one twenty-five, according to the speed gun—but Viktoriya jumped all over it. Her return was struck with such force it nearly knocked the racquet out of Laure's hands. Love-fifteen.

Viktoriya had spent most of the past two off-seasons training in Barcelona in an effort to improve her clay-court game. Rumor had it she had spent more time hitting nightclubs than lobs. Though she spoke Russian when she was upset about losing a point, she used Spanish when she celebrated winning one. A torrent of Catalan spilled from her lips as she sprinted to the other side of the court.

"Stupid, stupid, stupid." Laure admonished herself for getting away from her game plan. Placement, not power had brought her this far. Why change tactics now?

An acutely angled serve drew her even. Another one pushed her ahead. Thirty-fifteen. Two points away now.

Her string of aces ended on the next point, but she quickly took control of the rally. Appearing to tire, Viktoriya charged the net out of desperation. Laure coolly lined up a passing shot. Her forehand clipped the top of the net, slowly crawled up it, then fell back on her side of the court.

Laure held her head in her hands as the crowd groaned. If she had made the shot, she would have earned two match points. As it stood, she was still two points from winning. But now Viktoriya was two points from breaking her serve. And her spirit.

"Shake it off," Laure whispered as she waited for the crowd to settle.

But the mistake would prove insurmountable.

Viktoriya, recharged and firing on all cylinders, won the next two points to break serve. Then she held easily to push her lead to 6-5. Laure spent the changeover telling herself she was still in the match, but she couldn't shake the feeling she had missed her chance. Before she knew it, she was down triple match point and the crowd was begging her to pull off a miracle. Out of comebacks, she watched helplessly as Viktoriya's lob cleared her outstretched racquet and landed safely inside the baseline.

"Game, set, match, Miss Vasilyeva," the chair umpire said. "Miss Vasilyeva wins two sets to one, six-four, six-seven, seven-five."

Viktoriya's delighted shriek cut through Laure like a buzz saw. Leaning across the net, she extended her hand for the traditional post-match handshake. "Well played," she said automatically. Her voice was devoid of emotion, belying the feelings roiling inside her.

Viktoriya gripped Laure's hand and air-kissed her cheeks as if they were old friends instead of old enemies. "Thanks for the workout. Better luck next year."

Melancholy gripped Laure's heart so tightly the pain brought tears to her eyes. She bit her lip to keep from crying. *Not here*, she admonished herself as she zipped her warm-up jacket. *Not in front of all these people. Try to keep it together until you get off the court.*

She quickly packed her bags, but not wanting to seem like a bad sport, she didn't leave until Viktoriya was ready to do the same. As she trailed Viktoriya off Centre Court, she looked back over her shoulder as if she was seeing the storied venue for the last time. Just like Billie Jean King had in 1983. Then she knelt and plucked a few blades of the precious grass. Just like Martina Navratilova had in 1994. Like those two great champions, her Wimbledon career was over.

❖

The locker room attendant was crying. Sinjin felt like joining her.

"She's not coming back next year, is she?" the attendant asked. Sinjin shook her head.

"She has always been one of my favorites. Such a classy lady."

"She certainly is."

"She never has a harsh word to say about anyone. And I'm sure some deserve more than a few."

You don't know how right you are.

Even when Viktoriya and her ilk were at their worst, Laure never stooped to their level. Either in public or behind closed doors. Even now, when their relationship was more uncertain than ever, Laure had given her the freedom to make her own decisions. She had given her the room to find her way. To find herself. To find true love?

A tournament official poked her head into the locker room. "Thirty minutes, Miss Smythe."

"Thank you."

The last thing Sinjin wanted to think about was playing tennis. She wanted—*needed*—to console Laure. She turned to the attendant, who was discreetly blowing her nose in a monogrammed handkerchief.

"I know it's probably against the rules, but would you bring Laure in here, please?"

"Certainly, Miss Smythe." The woman's blue eyes sprang fresh tears. "She could use some quiet time after a defeat like that."

After the attendant left, Sinjin paced the room like an expectant parent. She kept returning to the exchange Laure and Viktoriya had shared at the net after the match. Whatever Viktoriya said to Laure certainly hadn't set well. Laure's expression had grown even more pained than the one she had borne most of the day.

The door opened. The attendant led Laure into the room. Laure's eyes were red, her chin quivering. The torment Sinjin saw in Laure's face nearly drove her to her knees. She tried to think of something comforting to say but couldn't find the words. When she looked into Laure's eyes, she realized words were unnecessary.

Laure dropped her racquet bag on the floor as her resolve finally broke. Sinjin spread her arms. Laure stumbled into them.

Sinjin held her as she cried, gently rubbed her back as powerful sobs nearly tore her in two. She didn't try to dissect the match or ask her what went wrong. There would be plenty of time later for *what ifs* and *if onlys*.

After what seemed like hours but was actually no more than a few minutes, Laure pulled away. "Thank you for this, but you've got a match to prepare for," she said, drying her eyes on her sleeve.

Sinjin rested her palm against Laure's cheek and tenderly thumbed away a stray tear. "The match can wait. Are you okay?"

Laure shook her head. "I can't do this anymore. I'm done."

"Are you sure? I know this was a tough loss, but don't you want to take time to think about it?"

"I gave everything I had. I'm physically spent. I'm emotionally gutted. I'm empty. I've got nothing left. No amount of time off is going to replenish my supply. I'm done." Laure rubbed her face with the heels of her hands as if she could scrub away the hurt. "But don't worry about me. You've got a match to win. And as soon as I get my press conference over with, I'll be there to watch you do it." She managed a smile, but the expression didn't reach her eyes. "Sorry I broke our date for Saturday."

"But we're still on for the Champions Ball, right?"

Laure's serious mien finally began to lighten. "I wouldn't miss it for the world."

She turned to leave, but Sinjin's voice stopped her.

"Laure—"

Sinjin hesitated, uncertain what to say.

"Yes?" Laure asked gently.

"Congratulations."

"For what? I lost."

"But you did it the way you do everything else: with dignity." She took a step forward. "I want to be you when I grow up."

She held Laure's face in her hands and gently kissed her lips. She looked into Laure's eyes, wishing she had the courage to say the rest of the words in her head. In her heart.

❖

Laure felt the pieces of her broken heart begin to mend. She placed her hands on top of Sinjin's to keep her from breaking contact. "It seems to me you're doing a pretty good job of being yourself. Why don't you keep doing that for a while?"

She left the locker room and headed to the Millennium Building to face the gathered media. She knew the forthcoming press conference would be brutal. She hoped it would also be brief. Sharing her innermost thoughts with a roomful of strangers holding tape recorders had never been her idea of fun. Neither was rehashing a gut-wrenching defeat. Now she had to do both.

She stopped by the tour leaders' onsite offices to prepare them for what was about to happen.

"I wish you had given us some warning. We could have held an on-court ceremony for you after the match ended," the tour chairman said.

"I don't want a going-away party. I want to leave the sport the way I came into it: with no fanfare."

The chairman gave her a warm hug. "I'm not going to say good-bye or even so long. I've seen you come back in matches before. I'm going to hold out hope you're going to do the same this time."

She managed a smile. "You can hold out hope. Just don't hold your breath."

"Don't you want to do something with your hair or put on some makeup?" the marketing director asked, holding out a bag of free samples from a cosmetics company tour officials were hoping to land as a sponsor.

Laure didn't reach for the proffered goods. She eyed the marketing director's shellacked hair and camera-ready wardrobe. "I don't have time for pretty. I want everyone to know how much this hurts. All those people who say women's sports don't matter, I want them to see how much it matters to us."

She walked to the press room and took a seat behind a bank of microphones. Her throat went dry when she realized what she was about to do. She opened one of the bottles of mineral water that had been placed on the table.

"Before we begin," she said after taking a long swallow, "I have an announcement to make. When the season started, I knew this would be my last year on tour. What I didn't know was that Wimbledon would be my last tournament and this would be my last match. As of this moment, I am officially retired from the women's tennis tour. It's been a great run. I'll miss everyone and I hope, on some level, you'll miss me as well."

"What are your thoughts on today's match?" someone asked.

"I'm obviously very disappointed about the loss. I had a good chance and I thought I was going to win."

"What went wrong?"

"I think I wanted it too much. In the beginning, I was thinking about the result instead of the process. I couldn't relax and let my shots flow. I got back in the match in the second set and managed to take the lead in the third, but Viktoriya played unbelievably well throughout. Her level never dropped. Her consistency made all the difference."

"What about the forehand you missed at five-four, thirty-fifteen in the final set?" someone asked. "Do you wish you could have it back?"

Laure knew she would be replaying the shot for days, weeks, and perhaps years to come. "No," she said with a wry smile, "I wish the net had been a little bit lower."

Sinjin lay on the floor and stared up at the ceiling as she took inventory of her body. She felt pretty good, considering how much tennis she had played in the past three weeks. Counting qualifying, she had already played—and won—enough matches to earn the title. But thanks to having to qualify, she still had two rounds to go.

A month ago, she felt like she was held together with spit and duct tape. Now she felt almost like her old self. Winning was truly the world's best cure-all. Modern medicine didn't hurt. She made a mental note to thank Kendall for being such a kick-ass trainer. Kendall's workouts had enabled her to play her best tennis when most thought her best days were behind her. And Laure was the best training partner ever.

Though she was taking the time to look back at what she had accomplished, she had to keep moving forward. How many surprise semifinalists had gotten to this point and failed to progress? Too many to count. She desperately wanted to add her name to the roll of past winners just inside the entrance to Centre Court. If she did, she would become a Grand Slam singles champion. Just thinking the words gave her butterflies.

"Two more matches," she said, momentarily straying from her mantra of one match at a time. "Two more."

"Miss Smythe? It's time."

Sinjin heard the nervous tension in her newfound friend's voice. The attendant wasn't alone in her apprehension. British fans had been down this road before. A player made a deep run, fostered hopes of a title, then failed to deliver. Now it was her turn. The odds weren't in her favor—the match in Miami was her only win over Chandler in six career meetings—but she liked her chances. She had already beaten three top ten players in the tournament. What was one more?

Hold your serve and you're in there with a chance. That's all you can ask for.

As she had feared, watching Laure's match had taken something out of her. But the kiss had put it all back and then some. She pressed her fingers to her lips, remembering the kiss she and Laure had shared. Remembering how hard it had been to limit herself to just one. She didn't need the dance music she normally listened to before matches to get her endorphins pumping. She was doing just fine on her own.

"Miss Smythe?" the attendant asked.

"Yes, I'm coming."

Sinjin gathered her bags and followed one of the tournament officials out of the locker room. In the holding area, she bounced on her toes like a boxer warming up for a fight.

Chandler watched her gyrations with a bemused smile on her face. "Before you ask," she said, plucking at the hem of her white tennis dress, "*my* wrist is fine. Do you have any other questions?"

Gifted with the same sarcastic sense of humor, Sinjin and Chandler had a friendly but prickly relationship. Sinjin responded to Chandler's jibe about gamesmanship with a teasing dig of her own. "How's the movie performing?"

"The reviews are terrible. The returns are even worse. The paycheck was good, but I think I'll stick to my day job."

"Smart idea."

"I'm the one who usually makes headlines."

Everything Chandler did made front-page news, sometimes for the wrong reasons. When the press wasn't talking about her latest dramatic come-from-behind victory or equally dramatic outfit, it was focused on her very active love life. In the past four years, she had been romantically linked to an actor, a rapper, a Saudi prince, and a racecar driver. Her current flame wasn't as high profile as her previous ones. She had been seen out on the town with a stunt man she had met on the set of her latest movie, meaning some good had come out of her cinematic bomb.

"Way to steal my spotlight this week," she said. "Mind if I have it back?"

"Why don't we share it for a while, say ninety minutes or so?"

"I was thinking more like sixty."

Chandler normally talked a blue streak after her matches but not before. Prior to a big match, she was as silent as a monk. Unless she was nervous.

Sinjin could tell Chandler's constant chatter was an effort to settle her frazzled nerves. She went along with the ribbing because the back-and-forth helped ease her anxiety, too. She loved the camaraderie of the tour, where everyone wanted to win, but for the most part, weren't willing to step on other players' necks to do it. Viktoriya was the exception to the rule. Then again, Viktoriya was the exception to a lot of rules. But Viktoriya's time was coming. So was hers. Maybe that time was now.

❖

Laure wondered how long it would take to put the loss behind her. A day? A week? Months? Or perhaps never. She had been able to joke about it during her press conference, but she couldn't stop dwelling on the forehand she had missed while serving at 5-4, 30-15 in the third set. If the shot haunted her this much while she was awake, how bad were her dreams—her nightmares—going to be?

She showered and changed before joining her parents in the holding area outside the Royal Box. As a former champion, she was granted lifetime priority seating in the prestigious section.

"You've had a wonderful career," her mother said as they waited to take their seats. "You're going to be remembered for your wins, not this loss."

Laure hoped she was right.

Her mother and father, along with Nicolas and Gabrielle, had sat in on her retirement announcement. She would be eternally grateful for their unwavering support. The four of them had been there for her whenever she needed them. Now it was her turn. The next phase of her life had begun.

She and her parents climbed the stairs that led to the Royal Box. A wave of applause greeted them as soon as they stepped out of the tunnel. At first, Laure didn't realize the greeting was for her. When the wave began to crest, she looked to see if Sinjin and Chandler were walking onto the court. Then the crowd began chanting her name.

Feeling unworthy of the adulation, she raised her hand to acknowledge the cheers and quickly took her seat. The crowd's sustained applause—and the hand of a tantalizing young royal—lifted her out of it.

Laure said "Thank you" to both.

Just as they had during her match, Stephanie and Kendall led the cheers. Gabrielle and Nicolas sat to Stephanie's right, Kendall to her left. Stephanie must have been wearing a nicotine patch because she looked to be the calmest of the bunch. Next to her, Kendall bounced like a Mexican jumping bean, filled with so much nervous energy she couldn't sit still. Laure knew the feeling.

The longer the tournament went on, the more expectations for and pressure on Sinjin continued to grow. Now the hopes of a nation sat squarely on her shoulders.

Laure's father leaned toward her after she sat again. "By the time the next match is over," he said, glancing at the distant member of the royal family who was openly ogling her, "are you going to have another phone number to add to your mother's refuse collection?"

Laure smiled, remembering the redhead from the National Gallery and the countless others like her who had sought her attention over the years. The prospect of a few hours of fun with them didn't compare to the promise of the future that lay before her.

"By the time the next match is over, I hope to have a return engagement in this seat to watch Sinjin play the final."

❖

When the match began, Sinjin looked to exploit Chandler's one discernible weakness—her movement. Chandler moved beautifully side-to-side, her deep ground strokes keeping her opponents pinned to the baseline. Her movement forward was suspect, however. So were her volleys. She advanced to the net only on her own terms, usually after one of her huge approach shots evoked a weak reply. Sinjin aimed to draw Chandler into the net at every available opportunity. Instead of zealously defending the net as she had against Blake, she intended to give it away. At least on Chandler's serve. When she had the ball in her hand, she planned to serve and volley on every point. She didn't want any rally to last longer than five strokes. The choppy nature of the match—old-school grass court tennis at its best—should prevent Chandler from finding a rhythm. If she could keep Chandler from settling into a groove, she would live to fight another day. If not, her inspired run would come to an end.

Chandler won the toss and elected to serve. The proud owner of the consensus best serve in women's tennis, she would be able to put it to immediate use.

"Let's go, Chan!" a familiar voice called from the stands.

Blake Freeman was sitting in the back row of the Friends Box, her parents on one side and Chandler's boyfriend on the other. Her hands cupped around her mouth, Blake continued to shout encouragement.

Not to be outdone, Stephanie followed suit. "Break her, Sin!"

Then the rest of the crowd got involved, each fan trying to boost the morale of his or her favorite player. Sinjin was the overwhelming crowd favorite, but Chandler's supporters made sure their voices were heard.

"Quiet, please," the chair umpire said.

Chandler bounced the ball on the face of her racquet as she waited for the crowd to comply. After a few more cheers, the fifteen thousand fans gathered on Centre Court gradually fell silent. Chandler stepped to the baseline, took a deep breath, and prepared to serve. The beginning of her service motion was slow and exaggerated, the ending swift and sudden. When her racquet made contact with the ball, the percussion often sounded like a sonic boom. She combined the force with pinpoint accuracy. Her second serve was less potent but no less a weapon, its high kick quickly bouncing out of most players' strike zones. Many players would have been happy to have her second serve as their first.

Sinjin knew Chandler wasn't going to be easy to beat. But if she held her own serve and kept pace, perhaps Chandler would begin to feel the pressure and miss a few of her first deliveries. Because of her height, Chandler's high-bouncing second serve didn't bother Sinjin as it did other players. She could tee off on it like batting practice—if she got to see one. Chandler was serving so well during the tournament her second serve was practically missing in action. No wonder bettors had made her, in her sister's absence and in light of Viktoriya's recent struggles, the odds-on favorite to take the title.

Chandler won the first point with an ace and let out the kind of growl she normally reserved for the crucial stages of a tight third set. Sinjin took the hint. She couldn't afford to work her way into the match. If she didn't match Chandler's intensity from the outset, she would be swept off the court.

Chandler got her first serve in on the next point, but Sinjin guessed right, hit a deep return, and won the point by steering a backhand winner down the line. She clenched her fist as she prepared for the next point but she didn't celebrate. No need for histrionics on every point. Just the important ones.

At 15-all, Chandler pumped in a first serve that registered one hundred twenty-five miles per hour on the speed gun. Taking a page out of Roger Federer's book, Sinjin blocked the ball back to get the point started. She responded to Chandler's crosscourt backhand with a slice forehand that landed in the middle of the service box. The short shot drew Chandler to the net just as Sinjin intended. Chandler got to the ball in plenty of time, but unable to stop her forward momentum, butchered the shot. Her forehand sailed well over the baseline.

Rattled, Chandler missed her next serve by four feet. Sinjin crept forward for the second serve, her heels just inside the baseline. She got the backhand she was looking for and went for a big return. Expecting another short reply, Chandler started to move forward before Sinjin started her swing. The pace of the shot took her by surprise. Caught in no-man's land between the baseline and the service line, her attempted half-volley found the bottom of the net.

"Come on," Sinjin said under her breath. Her quiet exhortation was lost in the roar of the crowd.

The underdog had a chance to go up an early break.

A good start was important for both of them. If Chandler could keep her nose out front, she could keep the partisan crowd quiet. If Sinjin got an early lead, the place would be bedlam.

Down double break point, Chandler took some extra time before stepping up to the service line. If she fell behind, she had it in her to come back—more than one opponent had taken seemingly insurmountable leads against her only to watch helplessly as she found her game in time to pull out the win—but she couldn't afford to press her luck. Sinjin was a dangerous opponent on most days.

Someone who made you sweat, but unless you were having an off day, wasn't a real threat to pull off an upset. The way Sinjin was playing now, though, if she thought she had a chance to win, she would take it. Chandler had to make sure their latest meeting wasn't a repeat of their last.

In Miami, Chandler had entered her third-round match with Sinjin looking past it to a quarterfinal showdown with Blake. Like the Williams sisters, the Freeman sisters hated playing each other. The ratings for the matches were always off the charts, but so was the emotional turmoil they experienced before, during, and after the clashes. For Chandler, having to defeat her sister in order to win a tournament, maintain her ranking, and keep her sponsors happy put an entirely new spin on the term sibling rivalry. At the end of the day, she and Blake were family. Between the lines, she was supposed to put family ties aside. Sometimes she was able to do so. When she was in the zone, the familiar face she saw across the net belonged not to her sister but a nameless opponent. Most times, though, she saw the big sister who had protected her, taken her under her wing, and taught her how to be a pro. Chandler led their head-to-head meetings thirteen to twelve, but Blake, better able to suppress the emotions that churned up whenever she played her sister, had won the last three matches.

Chandler had seemed almost grateful when her loss to Sinjin in Miami had prevented another set-to with her sister. That was the upside. The downside was the win had given Sinjin confidence. It had taken away Chandler's edge, the intangible advantage most top-ranked players had when they faced off against lower-ranked ones. That edge usually earned the higher-ranked players at least three games before play even started. Without her edge, Chandler was meeting Sinjin on an even playing field. And Sinjin had home court advantage.

Everyone watching seemed to sense Sinjin's self-belief start to grow. Where was the player who was always down on herself? The one whose game fell apart if she missed a shot or a call didn't go her way? That player had ceased to exist. In her place stood a woman who finally looked ready to go all the way.

In a hole despite being in a groove on her first serve, Chandler delivered a one hundred twenty-eight mile an hour ace down the middle. "Yes!" she shouted as if she had just reached match point.

On the next point, Chandler hit her biggest serve of the day. The speed gun flashed one hundred thirty-two. Sinjin's return was nearly as fast. Stepping into her forehand the way Andrew was always begging her to, she won the point with one swing.

The shot also won her the set. She easily held serve in the next game to stretch her lead to 2-0 and went on to claim the first set 6-4.

❖

The dominant serving evident in the first set continued to manifest itself in the second, neither player able to earn more than two points on the other's serve in a game.

After Chandler held at love to go up five games to four, the fourth time in as many games that the server had held without sacrificing a point, Laure got a sinking feeling in the pit of her stomach. Now was the time when Chandler normally made her move. When she snatched victory away from someone who seemed to be closing in on a win.

Sinjin hadn't been broken in the match—hadn't even faced break point—but if she lost her serve in the next game, it could cost her the match. Sinjin had fought so hard the whole tournament, her play improving by leaps and bounds each day. She seemed to be peaking at just the right time, but would it be enough?

"Well, well, well," her mother said. "Look who's here."

"Who?"

Her mother pointed toward the north stands. "Third seat, fifth row."

Laure counted seats until she located Viktoriya. Dressed in a tight-fitting T-shirt that said, "It's Good to be Queen," she seemed to be scouting her next opponent. Laure suspected she had something else in mind.

Viktoriya was safely through to the finals while Chandler and Sinjin struggled to decide who would join her. Chandler was too mentally tough to be shaken by Viktoriya's presence—or her studied calm. Was Sinjin?

❖

Chandler and Sinjin had reached the business end of the set, the stretch of games that separated winners from losers. In order to make the leap from competitor to champion, Sinjin would have to find a way to quell the nerves that always seeped into her body when a set reached its crucial stages.

Her twelfth ace helped quiet the voice in the back of her head. The one that tried to convince her she couldn't defeat Chandler two times in a row. Her thirteenth ace shut the voice up for good.

She raced through her service game to pull even at five-all. Chandler was just as precise on her own serve and quickly reclaimed the lead at six-five.

During the changeover, Sinjin took a couple of sips of water and quickly downed an energy bar. She wouldn't feel the protein-laden snack's effects right away, but if the match went to a third set, she would have the boost she needed. If she had anything to say about it, though, the match would end well before the energy bar kicked in.

She was out of her chair and on the service line before the chair umpire called time. Anxious to cross the finish line, she cautioned herself not to get there too fast. If she got too far ahead of herself, she would be mourning a loss instead of celebrating a victory.

She fell behind love-thirty, but before the crowd could get too anxious, served her way out of trouble and sealed the game with an unreturnable serve.

"Six games-all," the chair umpire said. "Tiebreak. Miss Freeman to serve."

The crowd yelled encouragement to both players. Most fans shouted for Sinjin to win in straight sets. Others, wanting a repeat of the thrilling first semifinal, begged for more tennis. Both players were eager to give the crowd what they wanted. While Chandler lived for the drama of a third set, Sinjin wanted to win the match as clinically and dispassionately as possible. With Viktoriya waiting to play the winner, there would be more than enough drama in the final.

❖

Though she loved the view from the Royal Box, Laure hated the close quarters—and the expectation that those seated there were supposed to cheer equally for both players. She forced herself to downplay her reactions to each point Sinjin won in the tiebreaker in order to comply with the unwritten rule.

"If this is anything like the set, we could be here all day," her father said. "Back and forth until someone finally breaks."

"That isn't going to be the case today. Whoever gets to set point first will take it. Either the match will be over in two sets or it's going to three."

She hoped Sinjin would be the one who reached set point first. If Chandler won the second set, she had the game and the mystique to steamroll through the third.

When the players reached five points-all, the crowd's cheers grew in intensity. Everyone knew how important the next point would be. The winner would hold either set point or match point.

Chandler stepped to the line and served a bomb down the middle of the court. The ball looked as if it had landed just beyond the service line, but the linesperson called the ball good. Set point, Chandler. Half the crowd screamed in delight, the other half in despair. Laure felt her palms begin to sweat.

Sinjin raised her hand in the air as if she were a student asking to be called on by her teacher. "Challenge."

The crowd, soaking up the drama, applauded the move.

"Miss Smythe is challenging the call on the center service line," the chair umpire said. "The ball was called good."

The challenge system was instituted two years after several egregious line calls cost Serena Williams her U.S. Open quarterfinal against Jennifer Capriati. The system was a hit with the fans and most of the players, who were allowed three incorrect challenges per set with an extra one thrown in during a tiebreaker. If a player argued a call and was proven wrong, she lost one of her challenges. If she was proven right, she kept her challenge and the point was replayed.

Some traditionalists disliked the encroachment of electronic line calling into the historic game, bemoaning the fact that the removal of human error lessened the number of controversies that brought much-needed attention to what had become, for some, a niche sport. Where would tennis be, they wondered, if not for John McEnroe's infamous tirades over missed calls? The more emotional players liked the fact that they could put a point behind them instead of stewing over it until it cost them a match.

Whatever their stance on the challenge system, it hadn't taken players long to learn to use it to their advantage. Some players disputed calls even when they thought the linespeople were correct. In those cases, the challenges were not made to correct an error but to disrupt an opponent's rhythm, ruin her concentration, or give her time to think.

Sinjin didn't get to use the challenge system often—the equipment was so expensive it was reserved for the show courts, venues where her matches were rarely scheduled. If she won this challenge, the ace would be ruled a fault and Chandler would be forced to hit a second serve on a crucial point, not an easy feat even for someone with her steely nerves.

The system operators played their part. When matches were close, they waited an extra few seconds to cue up the replay in order to add to the suspense.

Laure eyed the replay screen, willing the graphics to move. Finally, the system went into action, an animated ball slowly mirroring the flight of Chandler's contested serve. The ball landed less than an inch behind the service line. A roar went up when *Out* flashed on the screen.

"Second serve," the chair umpire said. "Miss Smythe has four challenges remaining."

At five-all in the tiebreak, the percentages dictated Chandler had to take some pace off her second serve to insure she got it in the box. She could be bold and go for a big second serve, but would she take the risk when the stakes were so high?

Sinjin settled into her service stance. Laure hoped she wouldn't blow her opportunity.

Make this count.

Chandler threw in a kick serve to Sinjin's forehand, her weaker wing. The ball sat up, begging to be hit. Sinjin obliged by rifling a wicked crosscourt return. Some fans whooped, thinking the point was over. Chandler's dazzling foot speed allowed her to get to the ball with ease. Her two-handed backhand was hit with just as much force as the shot that preceded it.

Laure looked on anxiously as Sinjin and Chandler played the kind of extended backcourt rally normally reserved for clay courts. The point reached ten strokes. Then fifteen. Then twenty. The crowd gasped in awe as both women chased down shots that looked like sure winners and returned them with interest. On the thirtieth stroke, Sinjin hit a backhand so sharply angled Chandler nearly had to climb into the stands to retrieve it. Chandler got the ball back but barely.

Laure leaned forward. Sinjin finally had an opening. All she had to do was slide the ball down the line and the point was hers.

❖

Sinjin thought Chandler, unwilling to concede the point, would race to cover the ad court. Not wanting to get burned by Chandler's speed, she played it safe and hit the ball behind her.

Too winded to sprint to the ad court, Chandler stayed home. The crowd groaned as Sinjin hit the ball right to her. Chandler cracked a forehand that instantly put Sinjin on her heels. Sinjin scrambled for the shot and threw up a defensive lob to give herself time to get back into position. Chandler hit an overhead as hard as she could. Sinjin chased the ball down and threw up another desperate lob.

Chandler had Sinjin on the ropes but couldn't put her away. Sinjin retrieved smash after smash as she fought to stay in the rally. Chandler grew visibly frustrated at her inability to end the point.

She finally eschewed power for finesse. Circling under the ball, she angled an overhead deep in Sinjin's forehand corner.

Chandler left her deuce court undefended. Spotting the opening, this time Sinjin made sure she didn't miss. The forehand was the hardest she hit during the match, the courtside speed gun measuring it at ninety-four miles per hour.

Match point.

Sinjin arched her back and roared at the sky. "Yeah!"

The crowd applauded lustily for several minutes, the respite giving each player a chance to catch her breath.

❖

"Quiet, please," the chair umpire said. "The players are ready."

Laure waited for Sinjin to turn and look her way. They had locked eyes as Sinjin celebrated reaching match point, but Sinjin had quickly turned her attention to the next point.

"Good," she said as Sinjin continued to maintain her focus. "Don't think. Just grab the ball and serve."

The chair umpire repeated her appeal for quiet. The crowd eventually complied.

Sinjin stepped up to the service line and began her routine. She bounced the ball three times, caught it in her right hand, and tossed it in the air.

Chandler looked uncertain. Should she defend her backhand or her forehand? Sinjin's kick serve to the ad court was her best serve, but she had hit only a handful of them all day, preferring to pick on Chandler's forehand or crowd her body. At crunch time, would she turn to her bread and butter or continue to mix it up?

Chandler guessed right but didn't get her racquet on the ball. Ace number seventeen took Sinjin to the Wimbledon final.

❖

Laure led the assault in the locker room as a group of players showered Sinjin with champagne and beer. The foam-filled bath usually occurred after a player won a title, not before. Sinjin didn't fight the break in tradition. Then again, she didn't have a choice. She was ambushed the instant she walked in the room.

"At least one of us made our date," Laure said, giving her a hug.

Sinjin wiped champagne out of her eyes. "Someone had to carry the flag for the Rainbow Brigade. Are you going to stick around for the final or are you going to yell at the TV screen like my grandparents?"

Laure gave Sinjin another hug. "I'll be right here. There's no way I'd miss the biggest party this country has seen in years."

"I hope I don't ruin everyone's good time."

Sinjin felt Viktoriya before she heard her, her sixth sense alerting her to the danger that lurked behind her.

"Is this a private party or can anyone join?"

The other players fell into an uneasy silence but formed a wall behind Sinjin, offering her their unspoken support.

Viktoriya smirked. "Then I'll be brief. It looks like I got what I wanted."

"Be careful what you wish for," Sinjin said. "It could come back to haunt you in the end."

"I doubt that. I wish you the best of luck on Saturday. I'll try not to embarrass you too much." Viktoriya turned and left the room.

The other players slowly drifted out, leaving Sinjin and Laure alone.

"Look at me." Laure turned Sinjin to face her. "Tonight, you're going to enjoy this win. Tomorrow, you're going to buckle down and prepare for Saturday. Viktoriya isn't the reason I lost today. I am. Despite all the head games she played before the match, I still had a chance to win. I simply didn't make the shots when I needed to. That's my fault, not hers. Don't make the same mistake I did. Don't underestimate your abilities and overestimate hers. I believe in you. I know you can win on Saturday, but it won't matter if you don't believe in yourself."

THE FINAL

"All set." Kendall squeezed Sinjin's left ankle as she pressed the last piece of protective tape into place. The layers of gauze and padding weren't meant to protect an injury but prevent one.

Sinjin flexed her toes and took a couple of tentative steps to make sure the bindings on her feet were tight enough to do their job without restricting her circulation. Then she sat and pulled on her socks.

The past forty-eight hours had been a whirlwind. Filled with interview requests, photo shoots, and other demands on Sinjin's time. The moment—the reason for all the hoopla—had finally arrived. The Wimbledon final was just minutes away.

"What's the plan?" Laure asked.

"I'm going to slice her to pieces. Backhand slice. Forehand slice. She's tall so I'm going to keep the ball low and make her bend as much as possible. By the time the third set rolls around, she won't have any legs left."

"Do you think it's going to three sets?"

"Straight sets. Three sets. I don't care if we play for one hour or three as long as I'm the one holding the trophy when we're done."

Kendall, Stephanie, and Gabrielle wore hand-lettered T-shirts. When they stood next to each other, the message on their shirts read, "Go, Sinjin, Go!" Laure, in a lightweight Armani pantsuit, felt overdressed.

"Good luck." Kendall extended her hand to Gabrielle, signaling they should leave. The locker room was practically overflowing with people. Kendall guessed—correctly—that Sinjin wanted time alone before such a big match. She and Gabrielle left to take their seats in the Friends Box.

"I have to go, too." Laure gave Sinjin a hug. "Play for yourself today, not anyone else."

Sinjin grabbed her hand. "Stay a little longer?"

Laure checked her watch. Her parents were safeguarding her place in the Royal Box. She needed to be in it before the Queen arrived. In a virtual murderers' row of dignitaries, she had been assigned the seat to the immediate right of Queen Elizabeth and her husband Prince Philip, who would occupy the place of honor in the middle of the first row. To their left, the prime ministers of England and Australia. Dozens of former champions were also in attendance. Martina Navratilova, Billie Jean King, Chris Evert, Margaret Smith Court, Steffi Graf, and Evonne Goolagong, to name a few.

Security was as tight as the players everyone was waiting to see.

Laure squeezed Sinjin's hand and sat back down. "I can spare a few more minutes."

She hoped Sinjin's nerves wouldn't get the best of her. Her hands were shaking so badly she could barely tie her shoes. She abruptly sat up straight.

"What's wrong?" Laure asked.

"I feel like I'm going to throw up."

Laure relaxed her grip. "That means you're ready. Before the U.S. Open final, you were laughing and joking like it was just another match. This isn't just another match. Your legacy's going to be on the line. Play like it. This is your moment, not Viktoriya's. Don't let her or anyone else take it from you."

Sinjin nodded resolutely.

Stephanie sat on Sinjin's other side. "I have something that should make you feel better. Do you remember this?" She reached into her purse and pulled out a keychain with a miniature replica of the women's singles trophy attached.

"Where did you find that? I thought I lost it years ago."

"I nicked it from you while you were packing to leave for tennis camp. I've been carrying it around ever since. It's been my good luck charm. Now it can be yours. Do you remember what Mum used to say?"

"'This might not be the actual Ladies' Plate, but one day, you'll get to hold the real thing.'"

The hair on the back of Laure's neck stood up as she felt another presence enter the room.

"Today's the day," Stephanie said. "I love you, sis."

"I love you, too." Sinjin's hands were steady as she slipped the keychain into her pocket.

"I'll see you out there." Stephanie gave her a quick hug before she left to join the crowd in the buzzing stadium.

Laure took Sinjin's right hand in both of hers.

They were quiet for a long while, absorbing the enormity of the moment. Win or lose, Sinjin's place in history was secured. She had backed up her appearance in the U.S. Open final by advancing to the championship match at Wimbledon. She was a Wimbledon finalist. No one would ever be able to take that away from her.

"A couple of days ago," Sinjin said, "you told me you believed in me. You said I needed to believe in myself. Thanks to you, I've found that belief. But there's something I believe in even more. Us. No matter what happens out there today, I know you'll be here for me. I was an arse for not realizing it before now. I'm sorry if I—"

Laure placed her fingers over Sinjin's lips. "Three years ago, you asked me a question. Do you remember what it was?"

Sinjin screwed up her face in concentration as she searched her memory banks. Her face lit up when she found what she was looking for. "Forgive me yet?"

Laure kissed her. "Ask me after championship point."

❖

After Laure left, Sinjin took a moment to compose herself. Her adrenaline was pumping so hard she could barely breathe. She pulled the keychain out of her pocket and ran her fingers over the intricate design. The raised inlay had worn down over the years, the gold plating rubbed off in several spots. Despite the trinket's battered appearance, it held undeniable power. She could feel its energy coursing through her as she held it. The real Ladies' Plate bore the engraved names of every women's champion since 1884. In a matter of hours, either she or Viktoriya would add her name to the list.

Laure had told her to play for herself. For once, Sinjin didn't take her advice. She squeezed the keychain and slipped it back into her pocket. Then she closed her eyes and lifted her head toward the ceiling. "This one's for you, Mum."

She grabbed her racquet bag, shook hands with her old friend the locker room attendant, and followed an official to the holding area. Viktoriya, fashionably late as always, arrived shortly after. Her white tennis dress looked as crisp and cool as she did. Sponsors' patches lined both sleeves of her warm-up jacket. Sinjin's sleeves were unadorned.

"The tournament referee will be with you in a moment," the official said. "He'll be able to answer any last-minute questions you may have. Good luck to both of you."

"How did you sleep last night?" Viktoriya asked after the official left. "Each time I play a Grand Slam final, I can't sleep the night before. I play these matches all the time, but it's been a while since you've made it to this stage. Three years is a long time between finals. I can't imagine the butterflies you must be feeling."

"My butterflies and I are fine. Thanks for asking."

Viktoriya's confident smile faltered for a fraction of a second. The moment was brief but long enough for Sinjin to register it.

"How's Laure? If I'd known I was sending her into retirement, I would have taken more time to enjoy the moment."

Sinjin smiled to counteract the spike in her blood pressure. "I'll give her your regards. If you ask me nicely, I might even save a place for you at our table at the Champions Ball."

Viktoriya rocked back on her heels as if she had been dealt a staggering blow, but she quickly regained her equilibrium. "Ah, Mr. Bloom. It's a pleasure to see you again."

Tournament referee Alan Bloom returned Viktoriya's effusive greeting. "The pleasure, as always, is mine." He turned to Sinjin. "Miss Smythe, congratulations for making it this far. You've managed to perform a feat no one has been able to pull off in over thirty years: you've compelled Her Majesty to attend a championship match."

"Glad I could help."

"Let's give her a show to be proud of, shall we?"

Alan gave each player a bouquet. In the championship round, the ball kids carried the competitors' racquet bags onto the court. The players didn't schlep anything heavier than an armful of flowers.

"At the insistence of His Royal Highness the Duke of Kent, the Club abandoned the tradition of bowing to the Royal Box many years ago unless the Prince of Wales or Her Majesty the Queen is in attendance. With that said, I hope you've been practicing your curtsies. When we reach the baseline, we will turn and face the Royal Box. The ladies will curtsy, the gentlemen will bow. After that, it will be business as usual. Any questions?"

"Just one," Viktoriya said. "What time should I arrive tomorrow?"

A few hours before the men contested their final on the last day of the tournament, the women's champion traditionally held a photo op for the press. Viktoriya's question let everyone know she fully intended to be the one posing with the trophy in the heart of London.

Alan coughed into his fist. "The, um, time and location for that event have not been determined as of yet. My office has your contact numbers, Miss Vasilyeva, as well as yours, Miss Smythe. We will inform all necessary parties when the information becomes available. If you'll follow me, please."

He led the players down the stairs. Before walking through the door that led to Centre Court, Sinjin looked up at the plaque affixed to the top of the doorway. The plaque contained a quote from the famous Rudyard Kipling poem "If," the work that urged the reader to meet with triumph and disaster and treat both impostors the same. Sinjin reached up and touched the plaque as so many others had before her.

"Wait here a moment," Alan said. He consulted his watch, waiting until precisely two p.m. to send the players on their journey. "Please proceed."

Viktoriya took the lead. Sinjin followed her into the bright sunshine. A roar went up as soon as the crowd got a glimpse of the players. Viktoriya waved her flowers over her head like an Olympian on the medals stand. Sinjin, fighting to keep her emotions under wraps, acknowledged the cheers with a similar but more subtle gesture. Then she shot a glance at the Friends Box. Viktoriya's friends and family occupied the second row. Gabrielle, Kendall, Nicolas, and Stephanie sat in the first. Sinjin had provided tickets for Andrew and her grandparents, too, even though she knew all of them would be too anxious to use them. Her grandparents were home waiting for her call. Andrew was probably pruning his roses or pacing in front of his TV.

At the baseline, the players, ball girls, tournament referee, and chair umpire turned and paid their respects to the Royal Box.

❖

Laure, seated between her mother and the Queen, joined the rest of the fans as they gave Sinjin and Viktoriya a standing ovation.

"We might be in trouble," her mother whispered as the players shed their warm-up jackets. "I don't think favoritism is allowed in the Royal Box."

"Then it's a good thing we're not royalty." Laure watched Sinjin, Viktoriya, and the chair umpire pose with the little girl who had been selected to conduct the pre-match coin toss. Viktoriya won the toss and elected to serve. "How does she look?" Laure asked as Sinjin jogged to the baseline to begin the ten-minute warm-up. "Does she look nervous to you?"

"No," her mother said, "she looks like she belongs here. You and I are the ones who could do with a change of venue."

Laure looked around the Royal Box. She tried to count the sea of famous faces but gave up after the number reached fifty. Agents from MI-5, ready to repel any potential attackers, occupied the aisle seats. To her right sat Billie Jean King and Martina Navratilova, the two women who shared the record for most Wimbledon titles with twenty. To her left, Australian Prime Minister Samantha Ogilvie and British Prime Minister Julian Firth discussed fox hunting with Prince Philip. Queen Elizabeth and Laure's father, meanwhile, were conducting a spirited comparison of the Kentucky Derby and the Royal Ascot Derby at Epsom Downs. Laure had no idea her father was a horse racing fan.

The Fortescue charm strikes again.

Before the first ball was struck, all things were possible. The match that followed could be a blowout, a classic, or just another routine contest.

Sitting in her chair waiting for time to be called, Sinjin tried to focus on the present instead of the past. *Don't think about history until you've made it. Until then, this is just another match. And the woman who looks like the Queen, she's just someone's grandmother.*

She looked around the stadium. British, Russian, and even a few Nigerian flags flew everywhere. Hundreds of fans held up homemade signs and posters rooting on their favorite players. In the stands below the Friends Box, a group of shirtless male fans had the letters of Viktoriya's name painted on their chests. Sinjin felt like she had fallen asleep and woken up in the middle of a World Cup match. She hadn't seen such an enthusiastic Wimbledon crowd since Goran Ivanisevic and Patrick Rafter contested an epic rain-delayed men's final in 2001. Playing on a Monday afternoon in front of a crowd composed of more Generation X-ers than club members, Ivanisevic had triumphed 9-7 in the fifth set to claim his last career title and his first Grand Slam.

Sinjin didn't know if her match with Viktoriya would stand up to the Ivanisevic-Rafter match in terms of drama and excitement. Relatively few matches could. When her match was over, she hoped that she would walk away with her first Wimbledon title.

"Time," the chair umpire said.

Veteran official Helen Rhys had been granted the honor of umpiring the women's final. Sinjin was pleased with the selection. Helen was one of the good ones. She supported her linespeople on close calls but wasn't afraid to correct a clear error. Firm but fair, she never tried to interject her personality into a match the way some umpires did. With her, there would be no controversial calls or ill timed overrules. She ran a tough ship, which encouraged players and linespeople alike to be on their best behavior.

After completing their last-minute rituals, Sinjin and Viktoriya took the court to another round of deafening applause. Analysts were torn on the importance of the first set. Some said winning the first set was crucial to Sinjin's prospects; some felt Viktoriya needed to claim it in order to keep the crowd at bay. Some said Sinjin needed to keep her nose in front to have any chance at all, while others said Viktoriya could easily come from behind.

Viktoriya looked across the net, trying to stare Sinjin down. Sinjin returned her glare. Viktoriya's plan to rattle her had failed. Unlike most of their matches, this one would be decided on the court, not in the locker room.

Viktoriya prepared to serve. Because of her height, she could lean into the delivery the way few other female players could. The shot routinely reached speeds unprecedented in the women's game. In addition to serve speed, she possessed machinelike consistency. She had been nearly flawless in the semifinals, missing just four first serves in the second and third sets combined.

Though she had watched only one of Viktoriya's matches during the tournament, Sinjin knew from past experience Viktoriya was going to be hard to break. She didn't expect to get very many opportunities. When they came, she would have to make the most of them—something she had not been able to do in their previous match-ups.

"Miss Vasilyeva to serve," Helen said. "Play."

Sinjin stood a foot behind the baseline, giving herself room to cut off the angle and time to make the return. As she always did before a big match, she tried to send a message from the very first point. If she won the opening salvo, she told herself, she would win the match. She won the first point with a textbook backhand volley, but Viktoriya rallied to win the game. Viktoriya extended her winning streak to six consecutive points by taking the first two points on Sinjin's serve before Sinjin steadied herself to pull even at one-all.

After shaking off their early jitters, they both settled down and put their game plans into effect. Sinjin sliced her ground strokes so finely they barely cleared the net. Viktoriya, meanwhile, used topspin to keep the ball deep as she tried to pin Sinjin to the baseline.

Viktoriya reached break point in the sixth game, but Sinjin fought it off with a good serve and an even better volley. Sinjin earned a break point of her own in the next game, but Viktoriya prevented her from taking the lead by threading the needle on a backhand passing shot that found the millimeter of space between Sinjin's outstretched racquet and the sideline.

"*Sí,*" Viktoriya shouted when her shot landed in the corner.

As the set got tougher, Viktoriya's exhortations grew louder. Sinjin, continuing to play well within herself, stayed mum. Tired of the mind games and backbiting, she wanted to settle her differences with Viktoriya once and for all. And she wanted to do it where it counted—between the lines. To do so, she needed to keep her head clear of the interference that crept into her brain whenever Viktoriya crossed her path.

At five-all, Viktoriya missed an easy forehand, her bread and butter shot. She yelled at herself in Russian, giving voice to the growing frustration she must have felt at not being able to put some distance between them. Excluding the match against Laure, she had trounced all her opponents in the tournament, losing an average of three games a match. But this wasn't just another match. This was the final.

After another error, the crowd prepared itself for one of Viktoriya's infamous tantrums—colorful tirades that had become YouTube staples—but she steadied herself and closed out the game to pull ahead six-five.

Channeling Arthur Ashe, Sinjin closed her eyes during the changeover. She tried to picture herself winning the next game and the tiebreaker. As Laure loved to say, if she could dream it, she could achieve it.

She took the first step by winning the twelfth game at love.

"Tiebreak," Helen Rhys announced. "Miss Vasilyeva to serve. Both players have four challenges remaining."

The first twelve games had been an extended warm-up. Now it was time for the real match to begin.

❖

Laure didn't subscribe to the theory that said the first set didn't matter. The set was already an hour old and had yet to be decided. After fighting so hard for so long, whoever lost the set would undoubtedly have an emotional letdown in the second set, meaning whoever won the first set would most likely win the match.

At nine points-all, the players changed ends for the third time.

"Careful. I need that hand to sketch with." Laure pried her mother's fingers apart, breaking the death grip she had applied to her forearm.

"Sorry."

Laure wasn't immune to the tension. She felt like a violin string that had reached its breaking point. In a few more bow strokes, she might snap in two.

Both players had reached and lost multiple set points. No, that was unfair. In the superbly played tiebreaker, points were won, not lost. Unforced errors were a rarity, winners plentiful. The crowd leaped to its feet after nearly every point as the players carved out impossible angles, hit offensive shots from defensive positions, and turned the set into an instant classic.

"Three guesses as to which match is going to be shown during next year's rain delays," Laure's mother said after Sinjin chased down a lob, overran it, and, out of desperation, hit a between-the-legs winner past the startled Viktoriya. "And the first two don't count."

"Neither will this set if Sinjin doesn't win the match."

❖

Sinjin tried to slow her racing heartbeat. The closer she came to winning the set, the farther away the finish line seemed to be. She tried to remain positive, but each set point that slipped through her fingers dented her confidence a little more. The pep talks she gave herself no longer had the desired effect.

You can do this.

She struggled to convince herself the words were true. Though she had never beaten Viktoriya, their matches had always been competitive. The razor-thin difference between them was Viktoriya's unshakable belief in herself. Her belief that no matter how many spectacular winners Sinjin hit, she would hit one more. The belief was innate, not manufactured. It had made her a champion—and prevented Sinjin from becoming one.

Belief, paired with three cold-blooded winners, helped Viktoriya secure the first set.

"*Vamos*," she shouted, directing her celebration toward the group of men who had her name painted on their chests.

"*Uno más*," they shouted back. One more. One more set and the title was hers.

Sinjin shook her head disconsolately as she sank into her chair. Her first lost set of the tournament was a heartbreaker. She wouldn't have minded so much if she hadn't come so close to winning it. In her head, she replayed the points that had cost her the set. If given a second chance, she didn't think she would have played them any differently.

She was just too good. But you can be better.

In the Royal Box, Billie Jean King and Martina Navratilova dissected the first set.

"Sinjin played some beautiful serve and volley tennis in that set," Billie Jean said. "No one plays like that anymore. It's a shame her effort couldn't have been rewarded. She did everything right."

"Except win the last point," Martina replied. "But Viktoriya looks like she's slowing down a bit, doesn't she? She was starting to labor toward the end of the breaker. All the emotional energy she expends even after routine points is bound to catch up with her eventually."

Billie Jean nodded. "It could bite her in the butt in the third. If there is a third."

"Sinjin's serving first in the second set. If she can hold her serve and sneak out an early break, she's right back in this. If it goes to three, I like her chances."

Laure, who had been eavesdropping on the conversation, broke into a grin. Sinjin's plan was working. If she stuck to it, she could still pull off a miracle.

❖

A lull settled over the court in the early stages of the second set. It was to be expected. Players and fans alike needed time to recover after the excitement of the opening stanza.

Sinjin easily won the first game of the set. When she changed ends, she sought out her friends and family for the first time since the match began. Gabrielle, Kendall, and Nicolas, who knew from experience the jumble of emotions swirling through Sinjin's body, immediately stood to offer her their encouragement. Stephanie followed suit. "You've got the heart of a lion," she said, pointing toward the sky. "Show it."

Sinjin turned to Laure. She had avoided looking into the Royal Box, afraid of being intimidated by the slew of dignitaries she would see staring back at her. At the moment, there was only one face she wanted to see. Only one face that mattered. Laure's.

"Right now," Laure said, her face a study in determination. "Make your move right now."

Sinjin stepped up to the baseline and prepared to receive serve. If she didn't break in the next game, it wouldn't be the end of the world. She would be fine as long as she kept her nose out front. Then the pressure would fall on Viktoriya's shoulders instead of hers. The pressure to keep up. To come from behind.

Some players fared better when they were ahead. Others were able to go for their shots only when they were climbing the mountain instead of standing on top of it. Sinjin liked operating with a lead. Viktoriya preferred to fight her way back from the brink.

In order to claim her fifth Grand Slam title, Viktoriya would have to do something even more difficult than coming from behind. She would have to come from ahead.

After winning the first set in a tiebreaker, she quickly fell behind 5-0 in the second. She held serve to avoid being bageled but Sinjin served out the set in the next game.

Gabrielle, Kendall, Nicolas, and Stephanie exchanged high fives in the Friends Box. Compelled by her surroundings into being more muted, Laure settled for a discreet fist pump.

"One more set like that and we can all go home happy." After watching Viktoriya smash her racquet on the ground, she quickly amended her statement. "Well, maybe not all of us."

❖

"Code violation. Racquet abuse. Warning, Miss Vasilyeva," Helen Rhys said.

Viktoriya shot daggers at the chair umpire with her eyes but held her tongue. If she received another code violation, she would lose a point. A third would cost her the match. Sinjin didn't think Helen had the guts to disqualify Viktoriya in the finals of Wimbledon, but after watching Serena Williams get tossed from the U.S. Open semifinals for her profane tirade, Viktoriya would be foolish to take the risk.

"Bathroom break," Viktoriya said through clenched teeth. Then she quickly left the court. A tournament official accompanied her to make sure she didn't receive any input from her coaches along the way.

The break wasn't against the rules, but Sinjin doubted its legitimacy. She recognized the ploy for what it was: Viktoriya's attempt to stall her momentum. She knew she had to be ready for anything. Viktoriya would pull out every trick in the book if she thought it could help her win. Then again, she already had.

Sinjin used the respite to banter with her supporters.

"I hope everything comes out okay."

"I'm so glad to see you're not too sophisticated for bathroom humor," Laure said.

"That was awful."

"Was it any worse than any of yours?"

"You've got a point."

As the break stretched on, the fans began to get restless. Anxious to see more tennis, they broke into rhythmic applause. Sinjin obliged them. She armed one of the ball girls with a racquet and, to the delight of the crowd, they played a few points. Sinjin won the first one when the ball girl dumped a forehand into the middle of the net.

"Choke up a little," she advised the blushing youngster. The ball girl followed the suggestion and, to the delight of the crowd, "won" the next two points. When Viktoriya finally returned to the court, Sinjin jogged to the net and shook the ball girl's hand. "Nice job."

Provided with a memory she would never forget, the grinning ball girl resumed her position on the side of the court.

Viktoriya's eyebrows knitted in rage. After her piss-poor showing in the second set, she was obviously in no mood for what she used to refer to as one of Sinjin's kind-hearted displays. Sinjin already had the crowd on her side. Now she had them wrapped around her finger, too. Playing patty-cake tennis with the ball girl had been an impulsive act on Sinjin's part, but Viktoriya glared at her as if it had been premeditated. As if Sinjin had done it to show her up. To embarrass her.

Sinjin could feel the fury rolling off Viktoriya in waves as anger helped her refill her rapidly diminishing energy reserves. Sinjin knew she would continue to add fuel to the fire. In Viktoriya's eyes, she had committed a cardinal sin: she had dared to have fun at Viktoriya's expense. Viktoriya wasn't about to let her get away with it.

As the third set commenced, the second set began to seem like an anomaly. Viktoriya cut down on the unforced errors that had plagued her in the second set, her level of play returning to the high level she had established in the first set. Sinjin's level had never dipped. In fact, it seemed to increase exponentially in each set. The longer the match went, the better she seemed to play.

Viktoriya hit the wall in the eighth game. She looked fine during the points. Between them, she looked half-dead. One minute she was limping noticeably as if her legs were cramping. The next minute she was chasing after balls like a gazelle.

Sinjin struggled to maintain her focus. Across the net, Viktoriya was doubled over as if she couldn't catch her breath. *Don't fall for it*, Sinjin cautioned herself. *She's just trying to play with your head again.*

But in the back of her mind, she wondered if Viktoriya's distress was real. Seeing her in as much pain as she appeared to be in was difficult to watch—and even harder to play against.

Up 0-30 on Viktoriya's serve, Sinjin lifted her foot off the gas when she should have pressed it to the floor. Viktoriya won four straight points to pull out the game, then called for the trainer.

Down 5-4 in the third set, Sinjin would have to sit and wait. And think.

The trainer, after taking several minutes to arrive on court, began her two-minute medical evaluation. At the end of that time period, she could ask for a five-minute medical timeout or defer treatment until the next changeover.

Asked to indicate her area of discomfort, Viktoriya pointed to the back of her right leg.

From Sinjin's point of view, Viktoriya's timing couldn't be worse. Or more intentional. Viktoriya's leg had seemed to be an issue since the fourth game of the set. Why hadn't she called for the trainer then? Because she wasn't a game away from the match then. Because at 2-all or 3-2, a service break was something Sinjin would be able to recover from. At 5-4, a break meant the match.

As the trainer worked on Viktoriya's balky hamstring, Sinjin tried to keep her muscles warm and her mind free. Thoughts of losing were not allowed to enter her head. She visualized her next service game, scripting it like a football coach planning the first quarter of a game. When she got to the line, she didn't want to have to think about where to direct each serve. She wanted to be on autopilot.

The physiotherapist wrapped a bandage around Viktoriya's leg and secured it with trainer's tape. Viktoriya tested her leg and the tape job. After performing a few knee lifts, she pronounced herself fit to play.

Raucous applause greeted their return to the court. Fans shouted encouragement to Viktoriya and Sinjin in equal measures, Viktoriya's apparent injury garnering her a few sympathy votes.

On the first point, Sinjin served out wide to Viktoriya's forehand to test her leg. Viktoriya passed the test with flying colors, rifling a winner down the line.

"*Sí*." Viktoriya clenched her fists and stared across the net to assess Sinjin's reaction to her shot.

Undaunted, Sinjin continued to follow her script. She directed the next serve to Viktoriya's forehand as well. Set up for a kick serve to her backhand, Viktoriya watched Sinjin's twenty-ninth ace fly by. The shot tied Sinjin's personal best for the most aces she had ever hit in a match.

The crowd erupted, but Sinjin didn't react. There was still work to be done.

Viktoriya's passing shots began to find their mark. Another huge forehand brought her to 15-30. A bruising backhand to 15-40. With Queen Elizabeth watching over her shoulder, Queen Viktoriya had double match point.

In the Friends Box, Gabrielle, Kendall, Nicolas, and Stephanie held hands, forming a united front. In the Royal Box, Laure and her parents did the same.

"It can't end like this," Sinjin said under her breath. "Not like this and not to her. You've been waiting for this moment your entire life. Don't let it pass you by."

She served another ace to save one match point. Then she waited for the applause to die down.

She knew she was taking part in a classic match, one that would be talked about for years to come no matter who won, but unless she pulled out the victory, she would never be able to bring herself to watch it. She didn't know which was worse, losing the match or losing to Viktoriya. Again. Neither scenario held great appeal.

She hit a booming serve and waited for a short ball so she could work her way into the net. Viktoriya's deep ground strokes kept her tethered to the baseline. Finally, fifteen strokes into the rally, one of Viktoriya's backhands landed close to the service line. Sinjin sliced a backhand and followed it to the net. The shot stayed low but landed short, giving Viktoriya a good look at the passing shot.

Sinjin's heart sank as Viktoriya drew back and loaded up her two-handed backhand. By protecting the sideline, she had left a sizable hole on the other side of the court. If Viktoriya's crosscourt backhand landed in, the match was over.

"Out!" the linesperson called.

Viktoriya raised her hands to her head in disbelief. "How did you see it?" she asked the chair umpire.

"It was on the far side of the court. I can't overrule my linesman. Would you like to challenge the call?"

Down to two challenges, Viktoriya couldn't afford to waste one on a point she might not win. But if she gambled and won, the trophy was hers. She waved her racquet dismissively. "Challenge."

"Miss Vasilyeva is challenging the call on the left sideline," Helen Rhys said. "The ball was called out."

Sinjin toweled off while she waited for the replay to appear on the screen. She thought the ball had landed just out, but she didn't know if she were seeing the ball with her heart or her head. She turned to Laure, who had a better view than she did. "In or out?"

Laure held up her thumb and index finger a half inch apart. "Just wide."

The replay confirmed her call.

"You promised me a bottle of champagne if I won," Sinjin said. "I think I'm going to need a whole bloody case."

"That can be arranged."

Sinjin fanned her shirt to show the relieved crowd her heart was beating out of her chest. The gesture drew a laugh, but Viktoriya obviously didn't see the humor in it. She was the best closer in women's tennis—and she had just blown two match points.

❖

Sinjin outplayed Viktoriya from the net and the baseline to pull even at five-all. A huge grin on her face, she soaked up the atmosphere as the crowd roared its approval.

Laure and her mother exchanged sighs of relief.

"You're right," Laure said. "She does look like she belongs here. She used to say she was going to play until she was thirty and then call it a day, but I don't know. Look at her. She's like a kid out there. She may keep going forever. Everyone dreams about going out on top. Pete Sampras won the U.S. Open when he was thirty-one and never played again aside from exhibitions. It would be incredible if Sinjin could do something similar—if her last match were her best match—but I don't know if she'd be able to walk away that easily. I know I wouldn't."

"I don't think I can endure matches like this for another five years," the Queen said.

Laure laughed. "You and me both."

❖

The most dangerous opponent was a wounded opponent. Sinjin had Viktoriya on the ropes but couldn't finish her off. In an epic game reminiscent of the twenty-minute, thirty-two point, thirteen-deuce affair Steffi Graf and Arantxa Sanchez-Vicario played in the penultimate game of the 1995 final, Viktoriya and Sinjin traded body blows for nearly half an hour. The game lasted longer than the entire second set.

On the forty-third point, Sinjin earned her seventh break point. If she won it, she could serve for the match.

Viktoriya rubbed her right hand. According to the speed gun, none of her last five serves had topped one hundred miles an hour. She had been serving so long her fingers were undoubtedly starting to cramp. Her arm muscles had to be screaming from overuse.

As the match neared the three-hour mark, Sinjin sensed something she had never seen in Viktoriya: vulnerability. Viktoriya's fans sensed it, too. They chanted her name, their voices accompanied by the sound of rhythmic applause. Then Sinjin's fans got in on the act. If the retractable roof had been closed, the din would have blown it off.

"Quiet, please," Helen Rhys said. Her request only made the crowd get louder.

Each time Viktoriya stepped up to the line, she had to back off because the fans wouldn't stop cheering. She turned her back to the court and wiped her face with her wristband. Just before Viktoriya turned away, Sinjin could have sworn she saw tears glistening on her cheeks.

"Quiet, please," Helen Rhys repeated. "The players are ready. Quiet, please."

The crowd reluctantly complied with her request. It amazed Sinjin how Centre Court could sound as loud as a football stadium one minute and as silent as a library the next. The onlookers were transfixed. Some clutched each other as if they were in need of comfort or solace or both. Some had their fingers crossed. Some had their hands clasped as if in prayer. All were ready to erupt.

When they trained together as teenagers, Sinjin and Viktoriya had often discussed strategy. Forgetting that Viktoriya could one day use the information against her, Sinjin had once confided to Viktoriya that, if given a choice, she would rather hit a backhand than a forehand. Her backhand was a formidable weapon. Moreover, it was reliable. Her forehand was sporadically brilliant but inconsistent at best. When she was nervous, she decelerated through the shot instead of hitting out like she was supposed to.

Sinjin knew where the ball was going even before Viktoriya began her service motion. Her forehand. No doubt about it. Even though she expected the shot, she still had to pull it off. She tried to swallow and she felt like she had a golf ball in her throat.

These are the moments that define a career. If you want your career to be complete, you've got to seize this moment, not run from it. Don't wait for Viktoriya to miss. Take it to her.

Her body and mind focused on what she needed to do, she stood with her heels on the baseline and settled into her return stance.

Viktoriya frequently pronounced herself one of the smartest match players on tour. Sinjin was the most skilled. Everyone knew Sinjin was a brilliant strategist, but her immense talent was often her downfall. When given a choice between a routine shot and a spectacular one, she went for the flashier shot every time. In practice, she could hit every shot in the book. Could she do it when the pressure was on?

Viktoriya's serve didn't have much on it, but it was struck with tremendous spin. Sinjin resisted the urge to take a big cut at the ball. To try to end the point with one swing. Exercising restraint, she blocked the return back to get the ball in play.

As they settled into an exchange of ground strokes, Viktoriya directed all of hers to Sinjin's forehand, trying to draw an error. The shot not only held up but began to pay dividends.

Ten shots into the rally, Sinjin's slice forehand landed just inside the baseline and barely bounced. Too leg weary to bend her knees to get down to the ball, Viktoriya bent from the waist and took one hand off her racquet to extend her reach. Grunting with effort, she barely dug the ball off the turf.

Sinjin moved forward to hit a forehand volley, the weakest shot in her repertoire.

Punch it. Don't swing.

Her technique perfect, she volleyed the ball into the open court.

"Game, Miss Smythe," Helen Rhys said. "Miss Smythe leads six games to five."

Sinjin was one game away from ending the drought.

Happily breaking the unwritten rule prohibiting cheering in the Royal Box, Laure and her parents joined the rest of the delirious Centre Court fans as they clapped, stomped, and chanted their way through the changeover. Even the Queen tapped a sensibly shoed foot.

While an exhausted Viktoriya sank into her chair as if she couldn't wait to get off her feet, Sinjin stood by hers as if she couldn't wait to get back on court. She drank greedily from a bottle of Gatorade as she tried to prevent the onset of the cramps that were threatening to form in her left thigh. Though she was sufficiently hydrated, nervous tension had her muscles in knots.

Her gaze lingered on the faces of her extended family. Gabrielle. Kendall. Nicolas. Stephanie. Laure. Even Henri and Mathilde. She wanted them to feel what she was feeling. The excitement. The anticipation. The pride. The love. Then she realized they already did.

The emotions she had kept in check throughout the match threatened to spill over.

"Time," Helen Rhys said, her unruffled voice adding an air of much-needed calm to the bedlam that was Centre Court.

When they returned to the court, all the cameras in the photographers' box swung in Sinjin's direction, their telephoto lenses poised to capture each moment of her march into history.

Sinjin and Viktoriya both realized how important it was to win the first point. If Sinjin won it, she could relax and roll through the rest of the game. If Viktoriya claimed it, perhaps she could plant a seed of doubt in Sinjin's mind and finally get her to crack.

Viktoriya got her wish. She won the first point with a topspin lob so perfect Sinjin didn't even try to run it down.

"*Vamos*." Viktoriya cast a long look across the net as she tried to judge how much her shot had dented Sinjin's psyche.

Undeterred, Sinjin played serve and volley on the next point and dared Viktoriya to pass her. The serve drew Viktoriya out wide. Her only hope was a backhand down the line. She had a small opening, but Sinjin quickly closed the gap and hit a backhand volley into the open court.

Fifteen-all.

A service winner brought Sinjin to 30-15, her thirty-first ace to double match point.

Viktoriya challenged the call on the serve, even though her body language seemed to say she knew the ball was good. Like her well-timed bathroom break, the challenge was her attempt to upset Sinjin's rhythm. To give her time to tighten up. To make her realize what she was within a hair's breadth of accomplishing.

Sinjin didn't bother to watch the replay. Toweling off at the back of the court, she waited for the crowd's reaction to tell her if the ball was in or out. She didn't have to wait long. The roar that went up made her eardrums vibrate.

"Forty-fifteen," Helen Rhys announced. "Miss Vasilyeva has no challenges remaining."

Her hands shaking as if she had imbibed too much caffeine, Sinjin took three balls from the ball boy, returned one, and examined the other two. New balls would not be put into play for a few more games. The old ones had taken quite a beating, especially in the previous game. New balls flew through the air faster, which helped the serve but hindered ground strokes.

Sinjin accepted the tradeoff. New balls might have helped her pad her ace count, but as excited as she was, one of her forehands might have ended up scattering the luminaries in the Royal Box.

Her excitement turned to trepidation after Viktoriya drew to within a point, thanks to her third double fault.

As Sinjin began to wobble, Viktoriya made an aggressive return on the next point. The serve was Sinjin's biggest of the match, topping out at one hundred thirty-three miles per hour, but Viktoriya treated it with disdain. Aiming for the sideline, she laced a forehand that traveled through the air so fast it seemed to improve on the speed of the serve that preceded it. The ball looked good when it left her racquet, but Viktoriya's stricken expression revealed she had slightly missed her mark. Leaning in the opposite direction of the flight of the ball, she tried to use body English to steer it back into the court.

The ball landed perilously close to the line. The linesperson hesitated then extended his left arm. "Out!"

The crowd exploded in jubilation then began to murmur in confusion as neither player approached the net.

Out of challenges, Viktoriya couldn't formally protest the call, but that didn't stop her from complaining vociferously to the chair umpire.

"You've got to overrule that call. The ball was on the line and you know it. It landed right in front of you."

Not having overruled a call all day, Helen Rhys was understandably hesitant to reverse the trend at match point. "The linesperson had a better view than I did. In this instance, I have to stick with his call." She reached for the microphone to announce the final score, but Sinjin held up her hand.

"I want to challenge the call."

Both Helen and Viktoriya did a double take. The fans closest to the court gasped in shock.

"You didn't have a play on the ball," Helen explained. "You do realize that if you challenge the call and it's reversed, you will lose the point."

Sinjin nodded. "I can't live the rest of my life wondering if I won this match on a bad call. I have to know for sure."

"Miss Smythe is challenging the call on the right sideline," Helen announced, her tremulous voice betraying her surprise. "The ball was called out."

The crowd applauded Sinjin's display of good sportsmanship. When was the last time a player challenged a call that had gone in her favor? Never. Though it wasn't against the rules, it put an unusual spin on the outcome. In a perverse twist of fate, if Sinjin lost the challenge, she'd win the match. If she won the challenge, she would have to serve at least two more points.

A sense of peace settled over her when the replay revealed Viktoriya's shot was good. *Win or lose, you did the right thing.*

Viktoriya gave her a look of grudging respect, but Sinjin didn't expect Viktoriya to be nearly as magnanimous when play resumed. She knew Viktoriya would do everything she could to make her pay for gifting her with a second chance.

Viktoriya pawed at the grass like a bull preparing to charge. They had played each other so often that no matter how much Sinjin tried to disguise her intentions, Viktoriya was usually able to predict what she was going to do. Usually. The thirty-one aces hinted she no longer knew Sinjin as well as she once did. But she still knew her well enough.

Sinjin got her first serve in, absorbed the power of Viktoriya's ground strokes, and worked her way into the net. Viktoriya hit a good passing shot. A great one, in fact. She hit the ball right in the sweet spot and her aim was true. When the ball left her racquet, she was certain she had won the point. Her fists were clenched in celebration and she seemed ready to let loose another "*Vamos.*"

But Sinjin guessed right.

Moving like Boris Becker in his knee-scraping prime, Sinjin dove to her left, cut off the ball, and, her body parallel to the ground, directed a forehand volley into the open court. She leaped to her feet and scrambled to the center of the court to prepare for the next shot, but Viktoriya remained rooted at the baseline. Her mouth agape, she stared at Sinjin as if she couldn't believe what she had just seen.

Sinjin had hit more spectacular shots, but never at a more important time. She noticed Viktoriya's entourage, who had obnoxiously cheered her errors all day, suddenly didn't have anything to say. Her supporters, meanwhile, leaped to their feet again, doing all they could to help her cross the finish line. They had come so far together. Now they were—for the third time—only one point away.

Gabrielle, Kendall, Nicolas, and Stephanie linked arms like the bench players on a college basketball team rooting on the starters during the final seconds of a tournament game. Laure and her parents gripped the railing in front of them, holding themselves back while preparing to lift themselves up.

Sinjin chose to go with her new favorite serve—the one to the body. Viktoriya, guessing wrong again, had set up for the kick serve to her backhand. Trying to get the ball in play, she ducked and hit an awkward squash shot.

Sinjin could see the ball spinning crazily through the air. She couldn't afford to let it bounce or it might go anywhere. Moving smoothly toward the net, she drew her racquet back and prepared to hit one of the riskiest shots in tennis—the swing volley. If her timing was off even the slightest bit, she would slam the ball into the net or club it a mile long.

She could hear Andrew's voice in her head reminding her of the proper technique.

"Pretend you're hitting a topspin forehand. Point to the ball with your off hand. Keep your wrist firm. Don't take too big a swing. This is tennis, not baseball. But when you hit the shot, make sure you hit the crap out of the ball."

She followed his instructions to the letter. The ball landed just inside the baseline. Viktoriya ran after it, but the ball bounced a second time before she had made it more than a few feet.

Sinjin fell spread-eagle on the ground as Helen Rhys called the final score. "Game, set, match, Miss Smythe. Miss Smythe wins two sets to one, six-seven, six-one, seven-five."

The sound washed over Sinjin like a wave. The sound of fifteen thousand voices celebrating the end of thirty-plus years of futility. The sound of her mother's voice whispering, "Well done."

Taking Viktoriya's feelings into account, she quickly picked herself up and jogged to the net for the post-match handshake.

"Congratulations," Viktoriya said, almost sounding as if she meant it.

"Thanks. You were a worthy adversary."

Sinjin pulled off her bandanna and tossed it into the stands. As three women fought for the souvenir, she shook hands with Helen Rhys and raised her hands over her head to acknowledge the long-suffering fans whose patience had finally been rewarded.

When the grounds crew began to roll protective carpet over the grass in order to prepare the court for the trophy presentation, Sinjin bolted across the court and climbed into the stands. Australian Pat Cash began the tradition in 1987 when he finally met the high expectations that had been heaped upon him by his tennis-mad nation. After defeating favored Ivan Lendl in the final, he climbed into the Friends Box to share the moment with his family. Men's and women's champions had been repeating the feat ever since.

Sinjin was flying so high she almost didn't need the stairs. She exchanged high fives with dozens of spectators as she waded through the delirious crowd and climbed into the Friends Box. She greeted Stephanie first, giving her a bear hug. "We did it."

"I put the ball in your hand," Stephanie said, "but you made the shots." She reached for her cell phone. "I've got to call Gram and tell her to turn on the telly. Her granddaughter just won Wimbledon."

As Stephanie placed an ecstatic call to Brighton, Sinjin turned to the rest of the troupe. "You guys were the best cheerleaders I've ever had," she said, pulling them into a group hug.

She looked longingly at the Royal Box. Decorum said she wasn't supposed to invade it as she had the Friends Box, but she wasn't feeling especially decorous.

Laure will probably kill me for what I'm about to do, but at least I'll die happy.

After testing the roof of NBC's broadcast booth to make sure it would hold her weight, she walked across it and climbed into the Royal Box. When Martina Navratilova and Billie Jean King shook her hand, she felt as if she were being welcomed into an exclusive club.

Then she spotted Virginia Wade.

"Thank you for making me something other than the answer to a trivia question," Virginia said. Though she had carved out an accomplished career on the court before going on to distinguish herself in the broadcast booth, to casual fans, she was simply the last British woman to win Wimbledon. Now Sinjin was the latest.

"I'm glad I could help."

She shook hands with Henri Fortescue and kissed Mathilde Fortescue on both cheeks. Then she turned to Laure.

Laure's heart pounded when Sinjin's eyes met hers. "You did it."

"We did it."

Laure laughed out loud when Sinjin picked her up and lifted her high in the air. It was the U.S. Open women's doubles final all over again.

"Kiss her! Kiss her!" the crowd chanted.

Laure glanced at the power players surrounding them. Her parents were watching. So was the Queen of England, for God's sake. "What am I supposed to do?"

Sinjin grinned. "I think you'd better do what they say. Unless you want a mutiny on your hands."

Laure bent and pressed her lips to Sinjin's.

Sinjin slowly lowered Laure to the ground. Her hands resting on Laure's sides, she allowed the kiss to continue.

Laure's hand snaked into Sinjin's hair, holding her in place. "By the way," she said when they came up for air, "the answer is yes. I forgive you."

She stood on her tiptoes and claimed her prize, one she valued even more than the trophy Sinjin was about to receive.

❖

Sinjin eventually moved on to accept well wishes from Prince Philip, Prime Minister Firth, and Prime Minister Ogilvie. She couldn't remember the last time she had shaken so many hands and received so many pats on the back. If she weren't careful, she could quickly become addicted to winning Grand Slams. When she turned to head back the way she had come, Queen Elizabeth cleared her throat. "Let's take the stairs, shall we?"

"By all means." Sinjin offered her arm.

Like her children, the Queen possessed a wry sense of humor not often on display. "Tell me," she said, taking Sinjin's proffered arm, "do you intend to kiss me, too?"

"Only if you ask me to, Ma'am."

They descended the stairs and parted ways just inside the entrance to Centre Court. Sinjin hurried to the sidelines to wait to be formally introduced as the Wimbledon champion.

The Queen made her entrance a few moments later, accompanied by the Duke of Kent. After they assumed their positions next to the table laden with the trophies, the public address announcer began to introduce the principals. Polite applause greeted tournament referee Alan Bloom, who was recognized first. He bowed to both royals, made small talk for a few moments, and briskly moved to the end of the receiving line. He was followed by chair umpire Helen Rhys.

"Ladies and gentlemen," the PA announcer said, "please welcome this year's runner-up, Miss Viktoriya Vasilyeva."

Viktoriya, her face puffy from unshed tears, walked on court to wild applause. She acknowledged the cheers with a slight wave, then displayed uncharacteristic humility as she accepted her runner-up trophy.

"From one queen to another, sincere congratulations on a most excellent effort. Shall we see you here again next year?"

"I certainly hope so, Ma'am," Viktoriya replied, her voice trembling with emotion. She held up her trophy but was unable to produce her usual megawatt smile.

Trying to pick up Viktoriya's spirits, the crowd gave her another rousing ovation. The moments after a championship final were incredibly difficult on the runners-up. Compelled to remain courtside when they wanted to retreat to the safety of the locker room, they were forced to deal with their roiling emotions in public. To relive the match. To replay critical points. To second-guess themselves with a crowd of thousands and an audience of millions watching them do it.

Viktoriya mouthed her thanks then stepped aside, ceding the spotlight she craved.

"Ladies and gentlemen, please welcome your ladies' champion, Miss Sinjin Smythe."

"We meet again," the Queen said, reaching for the trophy. "It is my distinct honor and pleasure to present you with this symbol of your achievement."

Sinjin burst into tears when she finally grasped the trophy she had waited twenty-five years to hold. She stepped forward to pose for the assembled photographers. As she held the Ladies' Plate over her head, she could hear her mother's voice whispering to her through the mists of time. *"One day, you'll get to hold the real thing."* The day had come. She tried to think of something to say during the on-court interview, but her mind was blank. Thankfully, Viktoriya would have to go first.

After the Queen left the court, former British player Sue Barker and her camera crew moved into position. Alan Bloom gently steered Viktoriya in her direction.

"Viktoriya," Sue began, "congratulations on an incredible match. Tough luck toward the end there. If not for a few points, you might be the one holding the Ladies' Plate right now. What was the difference?"

Viktoriya sighed deeply. Then she shot a quick glance at Sinjin, who was waiting to take her turn at the mike. "I threw everything at her but the kitchen sink today. She was just a better person than I was."

"I think you mean better player."

"No, I had it right the first time." Viktoriya turned to look Sinjin in the eye. "She's something special. I'm sorry I didn't realize that before now." She turned back to Sue. "She just won nearly a million pounds. Maybe next time we go out to dinner she can pick up the tab," she said, drawing a laugh from the crowd.

The public apology caught Sinjin by surprise. So did Viktoriya's playful wink. Had she finally won Viktoriya's respect? Perhaps today was the day they finally put the past behind them. Time would tell.

After thanking her agent, her fans, her coaches, and her parents for supporting her, Viktoriya waved to the crowd and, deciding the interview was over, returned to her chair.

"Viktoriya Vasilyeva, everyone," Sue said, covering for the abrupt end to the question-and-answer session. "Now let's hear from our champion, Sinjin Smythe."

Clutching the Ladies' Plate in her arms, Sinjin stepped forward.

"This has been a long time coming for you and the nation," Sue said. "How does it feel?"

"Even better than I expected. I've heard words like *magical*, *miraculous*, and *dream-like* bandied about for the past two weeks. All those seem highly appropriate."

"How did you do it?"

"I had a wonderful team behind me who believed I could do it even when I wasn't so sure. My coach Andrew Grey; my friends Kendall Worthington, Gabrielle Meunier, and Nicolas Almaric; my sister Stephanie Smythe; and, most of all, Laure Fortescue. Laure, you lifted me from the depths and helped me reach the pinnacle. I couldn't have done this without you. Thank you for being part of my life. Thank you for allowing me to be part of yours."

Champions Ball

Laure watched Sinjin pose for photographs with men's champion Rafael Nadal, who had put his own knee problems behind him to claim his third title. Sinjin's cream-colored suit perfectly complemented her caramel skin. She looked good enough to eat. The kisses they had shared earlier that day had been mere appetizers. Laure couldn't wait to get her first real taste.

Though Sinjin was obligated to attend the Champions Ball, Laure knew she would have preferred rounding up the troops for one last meal at the small restaurant she had frequented nearly every night during the tournament. The swanky black-tie affair at the All England Club would have to do.

The round table they had been assigned was filled with family and friends. Okay, family.

Nicolas, Stephanie, Kendall, Henri, Mathilde, and Gabrielle and her date each raised a glass to toast Sinjin's victory.

Applause greeted her return to the table.

"I've been smiling so much my face hurts."

Laure massaged Sinjin's sore cheeks. "Do your lips still work?"

Sinjin grinned. "Give me a couple of hours and I'll show you."

"I don't think I've ever slept with a Wimbledon champion before."

Sinjin draped her arm across the back of Laure's chair. "Then get ready because I'm going to take you on the ride of your life."

Laure reflected on the roller coaster ride they had taken the past few weeks. "You already did."

"Ready for one more?"

Laure had her answer ready even before Sinjin finished asking the question. "When do we leave?"

❖

Laure looked so good in her ocean blue vintage Chanel dress and jaunty Hermès scarf, Sinjin almost didn't want to take them off. Almost. She lightly traced a finger over Laure's collarbone, smiling at the involuntary shiver she caused. She reached around and unzipped the dress. As her tongue explored Laure's mouth, she pushed the spaghetti straps off Laure's shoulders and let the dress fall to the floor. Then she took a step back. Laure stood before her clad in a lacy navy blue bra, matching high-cut panties, and the printed silk scarf.

"You're so beautiful you take my breath away."

"You've seen me wearing less than this in the locker room."

"But I wasn't getting ready to do what I'm about to do to you."

Laure's lips curled into a smile. "What are you going to do to me?"

Sinjin shrugged off her jacket and tossed it in a nearby chair. "Everything." She picked Laure up and carried her to the bed. While everyone else continued to celebrate, they had returned to Laure's rented house, where they were blissfully, utterly alone.

Sinjin unclasped Laure's bra and tossed it aside.

Laure lifted her hips as Sinjin peeled off her underwear. "I'm going to come before you even touch me," she said, her breath quickening.

"Don't you dare."

Sinjin untied the scarf. Laure hissed when Sinjin slowly trailed the cool silk across her skin. Her hips rose off the bed. "As I was saying." A note of caution crept into her voice.

Heeding the warning, Sinjin quickly undressed and covered Laure's body with hers.

Laure ran her hands down Sinjin's back and over her ass. She squeezed Sinjin's hips and lifted her own, pressing their centers together. "God, you feel good."

"I'm glad you think so." Sinjin returned the pressure—and the compliment. "So do you."

She licked the hollow of Laure's throat, eliciting a soft moan. Wanting—needing to hear the sound again, she moved lower. Her lips skimmed across Laure's chest, sliding softly and wetly across the smooth skin until her mouth closed around one of Laure's pert breasts.

Laure's nails raked across Sinjin's back. Sinjin cried out at the unexpected but pleasant sensation. Keeping her eyes on Laure's, she moved to the other breast. As she tongued an erect nipple, she watched Laure's dark brown eyes turn almost black, her tanned face flush. Seeing Laure so free, so uninhibited made her want her even more.

She slipped her hand between their gyrating hips. Laure gasped when Sinjin's fingers massaged her swollen clit.

"God." Laure buried her face in the side of Sinjin's neck and nipped at the skin.

Sinjin threw her head back, enjoying the pleasure that bordered on pain. Then she kissed Laure's tumescent lips and slipped her tongue past them into her mouth. She groaned when Laure's tongue met hers, moving in concert with her fingers. She pulled away.

"Be with me."

Laure reached for Sinjin's hips and pulled her closer. "I am. I'm right—" Her eyes slid shut as she moved closer to the precipice. She opened them again after she gained some semblance of control. "I'm right here."

Sinjin shook her head. "Be with me."

She looked into Laure's eyes and waited until they were connected. She waited until Laure stiffened, shuddered, and relaxed. She waited until her own finely tuned body short-circuited and rebooted. She waited until the gathering storm had unleashed its fury. Then she said the words she had never uttered to anyone else. Anyone except Laure. "I love you. Let's make a life together."

"How?" Laure glanced at the replica of the Ladies' Plate resting on the nightstand. "What about your career? Today could be the beginning of incredible things for you."

"It is." Sinjin lay on her back and pulled Laure on top of her. She brushed a lock of Laure's sweat-dampened hair off her forehead. "It's the beginning of the first day of my life with you. So what do you say? Could a thriving young vintner use an assistant?"

Laure's smile was as bright as the sun. She eyed Sinjin's body. "I'll have to see your qualifications."

Sinjin gasped as Laure's hands skittered across her skin. Desire burst into flame, warming her inside and out. She reached for her. "You're the boss."

Cool Down

Saint Tropez
Several Years Later

Laure walked past a glass display case filled with trophies. Along with assorted other gold and silver cups and vases, three trophies from the U.S. Open, two from Wimbledon, and one each from the Australian Open and the French Open lay inside.

Clutching a bottle of wine in one hand and two glasses in the other, Laure padded barefoot to the backyard. Sinjin sat in a high-backed chair, her long legs stretched in front of her. In the distance, Nicolas and Stephanie held hands as they walked through the rows of grape-laden vines. Her parents walked alongside them. Her father, carrying Nicolas and Stephanie's two-year-old on his shoulders, led the way.

Laure placed the bottle and glasses on a small metal table and sat in a chair identical to the one occupied by Sinjin. She cut the seal on the bottle, inserted a corkscrew, and deftly popped the cork.

Sinjin held the cork under her nose and inhaled deeply. Under Laure's tutelage, she had quickly learned the ins and outs and subtle nuances of winemaking. Everything from the selection of grapes to the advantages of manual harvesting over mechanical. She couldn't yet identity a vintage simply by taste the way Laure could, but she loved practicing. Their business had taken off during their time together, both the vineyard and its production tripling in size.

Though business was booming, family life had never been more settled. Neither would have it any other way.

"Nice bouquet."

"Isn't it?" Laure poured the wine and handed a glass to Sinjin.

Sinjin swirled the rich, fragrant liquid and took a sip. "Mmm. Which one's this?"

Laure spun the bottle so Sinjin could see the vintage printed underneath the crossed racquets on the label.

"Excellent year."

"I thought so, too."

The label was stamped with the year Sinjin had won Wimbledon. The year she and Laure had become a couple. The year their disparate lives had become one.

Sinjin looked out at the horizon. The sky over their hundreds of acres of jointly owned property had taken on the hue of a brightly colored Impressionist painting. She held out her hand. "Another terrible sunset."

"I know," Laure said with a grin. She laced their fingers together, the gold wedding band on the ring finger of her left hand glowing in the light of the setting sun. "Maybe tomorrow will be better."

Sinjin held up her glass. "I'll drink to that."

About the Author

Yolanda Wallace is not a professional writer, but she plays one in her spare time. She has written two previous novels, *In Medias Res* and *Rum Spring*. Her short stories have appeared in multiple anthologies including *UniformSex*, *Body Check*, *Bedroom Eyes*, *Best Lesbian Love Stories: New York City*, and *Best Lesbian Love Stories: Summer Flings*. She and her partner of ten years live in beautiful coastal Georgia. They are parents to four children of the four-legged variety—a six-year-old boxer and three cats ranging in age from seven to ten. Yolanda can be reached at yolandawrites@gmail.com.

Books Available From Bold Strokes Books

Sheltering Dunes by Radclyffe. The seventh in the award winning Provincetown Tales. The pasts, presents, and futures of three women collide in a single moment that will alter all their lives forever. (978-1-60282-573-4)

Better Off Red: Vampire Sorority Sisters Book 1 by Rebekah Weatherspoon. Every sorority has its secrets…and college freshman Ginger Carmichael soon discovers that her pledge is more than a bond of sisterhood, it's a lifelong pact to serve six bloodthirsty demons with a lot more than nutritional needs. (978-1-60282-574-1)

Lucky Loser by Yolanda Wallace. Top tennis pros Sinjin Smythe and Laure Fortescue reach Wimbledon desperate to claim tennis's crown jewel, but will their feelings for each other get in the way? (978-1-60282-575-8)

History's Passion: Stories of Sex Before Stonewall edited by Richard Labonté. Four acclaimed erotic authors re-imagine the past…welcome to the hidden queer history of men loving men not so very long—and centuries—ago. (978-1-60282-576-5)

Detours by Jeffrey Ricker. Joel Patterson is heading to Maine for his mother's funeral, and his high school friend Lincoln has invited himself along on the ride—and into Joel's bed—but when the ghost of Joel's mother joins the trip, the route is likely to be anything but straight. (978-1-60282-577-2)

Holy Rollers by Rob Byrnes. Partners in life and crime, Grant Lambert and Chase LaMarca assemble a team of gay and lesbian criminals to steal millions from a rightwing mega-church, but the gang's plans are complicated by an "ex-gay" conference, the FBI, and a corrupt reverend with his own plans for the cash. (978-1-60282-578-9)

Mystery of the Tempest: A Fisher Key Adventure by Sam Cameron. Twin brothers Denny and Steven Anderson love helping people and fighting crime alongside their sheriff dad on sun-drenched Fisher Key, Florida, but Denny doesn't dare tell anyone he's gay, and Steven has secrets of his own to keep. (978-1-60282-579-6)

Three Days by L.T. Marie. In a town like Vegas where anything can happen, Shawn and Dakota find that the stakes are love at all costs, and it's a gamble neither can afford to lose. (978-1-60282-569-7)

Swimming to Chicago by David-Matthew Barnes. As the lives of the adults around them unravel, high school students Alex and Robby form an unbreakable bond, vowing to do anything to stay together— even if it means leaving everything behind. (978-1-60282-572-7)

Hostage Moon by AJ Quinn. Hunter Roswell thought she had left her past behind, until a serial killer begins stalking her. Can FBI profiler Sara Wilder help her find her connection to the killer before he strikes on blood moon? (978-1-60282-568-0)

Erotica Exotica: Tales of Magic, Sex, and the Supernatural, edited by Richard Labonté. Today's top gay erotica authors offer sexual thrills and perverse arousal, spooky chills, and magical orgasms in these stories exploring arcane mystery, supernatural seduction, and sex that haunts in a manner both weird and wondrous. (978-1-60282-570-3)

Blue by Russ Gregory. Matt and Thatcher find themselves in the crosshairs of a psychotic killer stalking gay men in the streets of Austin, and only a 103-year-old nursing home resident holds the key to solving the murders—but can she give up her secrets in time to save them? (978-1-60282-571-0)

Balance of Forces: Toujours Ici by Ali Vali. Immortal Kendal Richoux's life began during the reign of Egypt's only female pharaoh, and history has taught her the dangers of getting too close to anyone who hasn't harnessed the power of time, but as she prepares for the most important battle of her long life, can she resist her attraction to Piper Marmande? (978-1-60282-567-3)

Contemporary Gay Romances by Felice Picano. This collection of short fiction from legendary novelist and memoirist Felice Picano are as different from any standard "romances" as you can get, but they will linger in the mind and memory. (978-1-60282-639-7)

Nightrise by Nell Stark and Trinity Tam. In the third book in the *everafter* series, when Valentine Darrow loses her soul, Alexa must cross continents to find a way to save her. (978-1-60282-238-2)

Men of the Mean Streets, edited by Greg Herren and J.M. Redmann. Dark tales of amorality and criminality by some of the top authors of gay mysteries. (978-1-60282-240-5)

Women of the Mean Streets, edited by J.M. Redmann and Greg Herren. Murder, mayhem, sex, and danger—these are the stories of the women who dare to tackle the mean streets. (978-1-60282-241-2)

Firestorm by Radclyffe. Firefighter paramedic Mallory "Ice" James isn't happy when the undisciplined Jac Russo joins her command, but lust isn't something either can control—and they soon discover ice burns as fiercely as flame. (978-1-60282-232-0)

The Best Defense by Carsen Taite. When socialite Aimee Howard hires former homicide detective Skye Keaton to find her missing niece, she vows not to mix business with pleasure, but she soon finds Skye hard to resist. (978-1-60282-233-7)

After the Fall by Robin Summers. When the plague destroys most of humanity, Taylor Stone thinks there's nothing left to live for, until she meets Kate, a woman who makes her realize love is still alive and makes her dream of a future she thought was no longer possible. (978-1-60282-234-4)

Accidents Never Happen by David-Matthew Barnes. From the moment Albert and Joey meet by chance beneath a train track on a street in Chicago, a domino effect is triggered, setting off a chain reaction of murder and tragedy. (978-1-60282-235-1)

In Plain View, edited by Shane Allison. Best-selling gay erotica authors create the stories of sex and desire modern readers crave. (978-1-60282-236-8)